THE DIGNIFIED DEATH
OF
JOSEPH SHERMAN

R.T. Lawrence

The Dignified Death of Joseph Sherman

A Novel

Willow Ptarmigan Press
Anchorage, Alaska

ISBN 10: 0692564446
ISBN-13: 978-0692564448
Willow Ptarmigan Press
www.willowptarmiganpress.com

DEDICATION

To Laura,
my wife and best friend

CONTENTS

NOTE TO THE READER

This book is a work of fiction. With the exception of an introductory quote by Margaret Mead, the characters, locations, and events are entirely fictional. Any similarity of the story to actual events, locales, or persons, whether living or dead, is coincidental.

ACKNOWLEDGEMENTS

Many people have contributed to the hard work of editing and reviewing the multiple drafts leading to the final product you have before you. If you find yourself enjoying the book, I want you to be aware of some of the people to whom you and I are both indebted:

Laura Lawrence, M.Ed., my wife, editor, and source of perseverance throughout the sometimes tedious writing process.

Michael Justus, MD, whose wisdom as a physician and encourager provided the inspiration for turning a simple story into a parable.

Degnan Lawrence, my son whose review and advice regarding good writing and a cover design have been invaluable.

Sheila Vamplin, M.A., LMFT, whose gentle guidance helped enrich the story for a broad audience.

Laura Brooks, M.S., LPA, who added details to the story that deepened the presentation of medical care within a state correctional institution.

Larry Long, Ph.D, whose undergraduate writing class, which I took twenty years ago, continues to influence everything I write.

Eugene Underwood, Ed.D., and **John Williams, Ph.D**, whose literary guidance brought the narrative of so many of these characters to life.

John Patrick, MD, whose lectures and writing introduced foundational ideas for the encounters in this story.

Arthur F. Holmes, Ph.D, whose philosophical lectures provided ancient voices for this modern work of fiction.

INTRODUCTION

"For the first time in our tradition there was a complete separation between killing and curing. Throughout the primitive world the doctor and the sorcerer tended to be the same person. He with power to kill had power to cure, including specially the undoing of his own killing activities. He who had power to cure would necessarily also be able to kill. With the Greeks, the distinction was made clear. One profession, the followers of Asclepius, were to be dedicated completely to life under all circumstances, regardless of rank, age, or intellect--the life of a slave, the life of the Emperor, the life of a foreign man, the life of a defective child...this is a priceless possession which we cannot afford to tarnish, but society always is attempting to make the physician into a killer—to kill the defective child at birth, to leave the sleeping pills beside the bed of the cancer patient...it is the duty of society to protect the physician from such requests."

Margaret Mead quoted by Maurice Levine, MD.
Levine, Maurice. *Psychiatry and Ethics*. New York: G Braziller. 1972. pp. 324-325

PROLOGUE

PURSUING AND BEING PURSUED

"I thought the guy was on death's doorstep. Is he just feigning the whole illness?"

- Lieutenant John Burke
Department of Corrections

Avalyn Robbins burst through the door into the bright, open air. She held a hand above her forehead, squinting against the sunlight and scanning the tree-lined park with its mixed scents of fresh-cut grass and blooming flowers. She looked for any sign of Lieutenant Burke or Joseph Sherman.

The park was filled with a mix of laughter, shouts, nearby traffic noise, and chirping birds. But the two men, one pursuing, the other being pursued, were not immediately visible.

Avalyn held an emergency bag firmly on her shoulder. She felt nervous energy in her legs and chest, like a runner before the starting gun; she was ready to sprint but unclear about which direction she should run. She could see a crowd ahead of her gathered in the center of the park.

She walked in the direction of the crowd. Pedestrians and joggers wove past her, moving in both directions; they seemed distant, oblivious to the possible presence of a killer in their midst.

Avalyn scanned the crowd. She looked intently at the details of each face and anxiously bounced on her toes to see above and then beyond the people on the edge of the crowd. *Where is he?* She derided herself for not having moved faster.

Suddenly she felt a firm hand on her shoulder. She spun to see Lieutenant Burke standing behind her with a finger raised against his lips to indicate she should remain silent. He spoke in a hushed tone while looking around them, "I thought I said stay put. Sherman is somewhere

here in the park. I saw him run toward this sideshow, but I lost him in the crowd. Follow me and keep your eyes open."

The two of them walked up to a grass-covered rise on the park lawn from which they could view the entire park. Avalyn watched people pass for several minutes; suddenly, something caught her attention. She bumped the lieutenant with her elbow and pointed toward a man seated on a bench with his back to them. He was sitting about two hundred yards away. She noticed the man was dressed in blue, leaning forward, holding what appeared to be a hat in his hands.

"It could be Sherman," said the lieutenant. He immediately but quietly edged toward the seated gentleman with a hand held over his holstered weapon as if ready to draw.

Avalyn was not so reserved. Either due to nerves or the general excitement of the moment, she cupped her hands over her mouth and yelled out, "Sherman!"

At first, no one seemed to hear her. The attention of the crowd was not swayed from the street performers, and pedestrians continued to walk past, unresponsive to Avalyn's call. But the man on the bench slowly placed an arm up on the back of the bench and turned to look. Avalyn thought, *Even in the crowded din of a city park a man cannot resist the sound of his own name. We caught you, Sherman.*

Sherman first looked back toward the grass atop which Avalyn stood. His attention quickly shifted toward the lieutenant, who was now running toward him.

Sherman sprang to his feet. He held out his hat and bowed toward both Avalyn and Lieutenant Burke in a manner that acknowledged his pursuers and bid them farewell. Then he placed the hat on his head and ran into the crowd.

Avalyn did not give chase. She stood on the grass-covered rise from which she could see Lieutenant Burke follow Sherman into the crowd. She lost them in the midst of people but could discern their position by watching the movement of individuals erratically shifting to get out of the way, much like watching two people running through a corn field.

Avalyn saw Sherman break free on the far side of the crowd.

Seconds later, Lieutenant Burke rushed out of the crowd and bolted toward Sherman in a full sprint with his weapon drawn shouting, "Sherman! Stop where you are!"

Avalyn watched as Sherman wove his way around several lanes of traffic on the distant edge of the park, skillfully disappearing behind a bus stop. It was here that the lieutenant lost Sherman.

Avalyn peered forward. She reflexively held both hands over the sides of her eyes in order to get a clear view. She could see Lieutenant Burke pacing back and forth, looking across the street. Neither of them could see Sherman.

After several minutes Lieutenant Burke raised his arms in frustration. He turned and walked back toward Avalyn, who, seeing the lieutenant coming toward her, picked up the emergency bag she had lowered to the ground and walked toward him as well. They met in front of the park bench where Sherman had just been sitting. The lieutenant reclined onto the bench, still breathless from the pursuit. He leaned his head back toward the sky and reprimanded Avalyn, "What were you thinking, Robbins. I was so close. Don't they teach you nurses when to keep your mouth shut? I'll take care of security. You stick to medical care. Got it?"

"I'm really sorry, Lieutenant. I reacted without

thinking. I did not think he'd up and run."

Avalyn dropped her bag to the ground and took a seat next to the lieutenant. She avoided the urge to speak further.

Lieutenant Burke leaned forward with his hands on his knees as he scanned the park. He continued to breathe heavily, his mouth open, gulping large mouthfuls of air.

Lieutenant Burke wiped the beads of sweat from his forehead and turned to Avalyn, "Explain to me how a prisoner with serious medical problems can run like that. Look at me. I can't get my breath. My legs feel like gelatin. My knees are on fire. But my doc says I'm still in my prime. How could Sherman outrun me? I thought the guy was on death's doorstep. Is he just feigning the whole illness?"

Avalyn shook her head, but she did not immediately answer. She leaned back on the bench and looked up into the beams of light pouring through the intertwined limbs and leaves of the large park trees. The bench gave her body a chance to rest, but her mind raced through the events of the day. *How could this escaped prisoner pull one woman's heart so wildly in so many directions?*

CHAPTER ONE

PRISONER AWARDED THE RIGHT TO DIE

"I have been diagnosed with a terminal illness and wish to avoid prolonged suffering."

-Joseph E. Sherman
Prison Inmate

The unwelcome beeping of an alarm clock woke Avalyn from her deep, desperately needed restorative sleep.

Incremental waves of adrenaline and cortisol pulsed through her somnolent arteries, recalibrating her body for the time-bound world of consciousness. She blindly slapped at the alarm and reached for her glasses. The clock read five AM.

Avalyn glanced across the bed at her sleeping husband. He remained in a deep sleep, unmoved by the alarm. She fought the desire to wake him. *Not now*, she thought; *it is his turn to sleep.*

He was a corrections officer, and Avalyn was a prison nurse. They had met several years earlier, working at the same state corrections facility.

Avalyn propped herself on one elbow and watched her husband sleeping, his chest rising and falling as if in time with the slow brain waves of sleep. Even in sleep, he made her feel safe, protected from the waiting stresses of the day. For some reason, the moment brought back memories of the day they first met.

When she was new to the nursing profession, only a few months out of school, passing medication in a mental health wing of the prison, she was attacked by a prisoner. An inmate with a profound mental illness had pushed her to the floor in a delusional attempt to escape his cell.

The inmate was instantly restrained by a young muscular, square-jawed officer in a blue uniform, also new to his profession.

On that day, a new relationship began; the young officer and Avalyn became friends. Over time that friendship grew into romance and, even after the glow of new love dimmed, their romance transitioned into something more enduring.

He made her feel safe. As strange as it sounds, she felt secure anywhere in the prison as long as he was on duty. The inmates nicknamed him the Rock; he knew the games criminals play, and he maintained a suppressive eye on the players. He was respected by even hardened criminals for being firm, fair, and consistent.

Inmates spoke of Avalyn in secret as Robbins' girl, and this made her untouchable. She and Officer Robbins dated briefly and then married.

For a number of years, they worked together on the same shifts, at least until the first child was born. Then Avalyn stayed home. After a second child was born, Avalyn went back to work. She and her young husband began alternating week-on-week-off schedules to share the balance between work and parenting.

It was now Avalyn's week to go to work. She stared pensively across the bed at her sleeping husband, allowing her mind to wander between thoughts of the past and future. She missed going to work with her champion. But in a few hours, two toddlers full of energy and life would be awake and ready for new adventures. "They need you more," she whispered. So Avalyn left her husband to rest in preparation for his own day, whispering, "Rest well, my hero."

After brewing a cup of coffee and preparing breakfast, she sat down at the kitchen table to review the morning news.

A particular headline caught her eye. She grimaced and shook her head. Her hand trembled, causing coffee to spill over from her cup as she lowered it to the saucer without looking away from the article.

She read the column slowly, studying it carefully, "A federal court grants a convicted murderer the right to die at his own hands."

The article gave a brief history of the controversy. The state legislature passed what was termed the Death with Dignity Act, which allowed patients who were diagnosed with a terminal illness the right to voluntarily terminate their own lives. Six months after the legislation passed, an inmate named Joseph Sherman filed a lawsuit against the state department of corrections because, as a prisoner, he had been denied a request to terminate his own life.

In every way, Sherman met the criteria for participation under the state's Death with Dignity Act. He had been diagnosed with a terminal form of cancer. He was reasonably expected to die from the cancer within six months, and his prison physician, who determined Sherman to be mentally competent, agreed to prescribe a lethal dose of medication.

But the process was stopped by the governor. In response to public outcry, including allegations of creating a subversive system of capital punishment for sick inmates, and in response to personal petitions by multiple legislators who said their constituents complained of victims' rights being violated, the governor issued an executive order stopping the process.

Joseph Sherman immediately filed a lawsuit in federal court. His attorneys argued that Mr. Sherman was serving a life sentence without parole. He would die in prison, regardless. The unnecessary prolongation of what was sure to be a painful death, they argued, was a clear violation of Mr. Sherman's Eighth Amendment rights against cruel and unusual punishment.

Experts in medicine, law, and ethics lined up on both sides of the issue. Some argued that physician-assisted death was a part of the continuum of compassionate health care to which all inmates have a right. Others argued that the corrections system cannot be involved in the practice of taking life. Both sides agreed that the state must take into account the victims of crime, victims' families, and public safety.

After months of debate, expedited to some extent because of Mr. Sherman's terminal illness, a federal court determined that Mr. Sherman's right to autonomy superseded the State's peniological interests in prolonging the life of a convicted individual who was expected to die from an illness unrelated to the crimes for which he was incarcerated.

Put simply, Mr. Sherman retained the right to die on his own terms.

Avalyn had largely ignored the debate. Politics was the

ball and chain of her administrators. She saw herself as a professional nurse, serving a supporting role on the stage of health care; the weight of responsibility for the actual script fell to her superiors. She was a patient advocate and dispenser of care, care that was largely ordered by others. But as she read the article she felt a suffocating tightness welling in her throat. The debate had come to her door like an imposing salesman; the reality of actively helping someone die had never crossed her mind, and now the issue sat blatantly before her, pressing her to sign on.

Avalyn began to rub her temples. She posed a rhetorical question to an otherwise empty kitchen table, "Do they know who this guy is?" She knew Mr. Sherman well, maybe too well. Joseph Sherman was not just an inmate in the prison, he was her patient.

Sherman was serving multiple life sentences for the murders of at least five people, some of them young women. The crimes had been committed decades before, and Sherman was now an older man, strong still, but with declining health.

Avalyn first met Sherman when he was moved to the prison infirmary; she was his nurse the day he received the diagnosis of an inoperable metastatic cancer.

Avalyn thought back to that surreal moment when the prison doctor walked out of Joseph Sherman's cell. As the doctor passed Avalyn he raised his arms impatiently, "What more can I say? He's a dead man."

Avalyn heard the doctor's words. She remembered standing speechless. How could a physician say such a thing in front of the patient? She wanted to react, to advocate for this patient she did not yet know, but at the time she could not speak.

Her reluctance was not a reflection of cowardice or incompetence; she knew enough to conclude the doctor was probably correct. Joseph Sherman was crossing over from life to death, but she thought surely there was a better way to disclose such information to a person diagnosed with a terrible disease.

She remembered Sherman's first question. He was lying in a weakened state, slightly pale from a combination of anemia and the shock of having received grim news, "Nurse Robbins, what does it mean to be free?"

"Free from what?" Avalyn had asked.

"Free from fear. Free from external controls. Free from everyone else making decisions. What does that feel like? Please remind me; I have forgotten. What is it like to walk out that door each day and breathe free air? What is it like to hear a siren and have no fear? What is it like to choose what you will eat for dinner or where you will go on a trip? Tell me. Is freedom worth it? They say freedom comes to those who follow the rules; but following another man's rules is not freedom, it's slavery; it's tyranny. Is freedom worth such oppression?"

"I am a nurse, Mr. Sherman, not a philosopher. I don't even know how to answer your questions. But I am curious what makes you ask such things?"

"You heard the doctor, I'm a dead man. My time is up. I did not choose the day of my birth. Am I now free to choose the day of my death? No, of course not, that too has been taken from me."

Avalyn nodded but did not speak.

Sherman looked at her and continued, "I want to feel freedom one last time. To make a decision and know, right or wrong, it was my choice and mine alone."

"What are you saying Mr. Sherman? Are you thinking of doing something rash?"

Sherman had laughed, "Maybe. I'm a dead man; you heard the doc. What do I have to lose? I'm not scared of much, Nurse Robbins, but the idea of dying in this place terrifies me."

"What are you planning to do?"

"That's a private matter. I just need out. Surely a dying man has options. Doesn't the law make accommodations for the terminally ill?"

"What makes you afraid of passing here?"

"You want to know the truth? You want to know what really scares me? I am afraid I will die and never see my child again."

"You have children?"

"Just one, a daughter. How about you? Do you have children, Nurse Robbins? What if you thought you'd never see them again. Would that not cause you fear?"

"Mr. Sherman, we can contact your daughter or other family if you wish."

"It's no use. You will never be able to contact her. And at this point, it does not matter."

Avalyn initially felt compassion for Joseph Sherman, but even during that first conversation, she wondered whether Sherman, like many inmates, was using his new diagnosis as a lever for outmaneuvering the penal system. He did not seem so concerned about the fact that he was dying. Rather, he appeared to be contemplating ways to use this new information to his advantage.

Avalyn had walked away from the meeting with Mr. Sherman and had written a message in his medical chart, "The patient has received a terminal diagnosis and wishes to discuss options for release."

She did not concern herself with the ethics of that discussion. A list of others, the doctor, Sherman's attorney, the parole board, and a host of other people would bear the weight of responsibility for any decisions made. Her job was merely to make the patient's wishes known.

She had largely ignored the debate since that day; her priorities pulled her in other directions. While she was working, she cared for dozens of inmates. As a devoted wife and mother, she cared attentively for two toddlers and a husband while at home.

Until that day, Joseph Sherman and his medical problems had only occupied a small corner of Avalyn's working world; she delivered his medication daily, and at Sherman's request, she had read over his application for a medical parole, but his concerns never followed her home.

To the public, however, Sherman became somewhat of a celebrity. Like some serial killers, he developed a cult following both inside and outside the prison. A best-selling author wrote a book about his crimes and his capture, which was shot into a blockbuster movie starring

A-list actors, many of whom came to visit Mr. Sherman in prison. He enjoyed the attention; to a large degree he demonstrated great skill in using the media to craft his own personal legacy.

At the sight of Sherman on the front page, Avalyn shook her head. *Mr. Sherman has an affinity for the dramatic*, she thought. *It is only fitting for him to grab the spotlight one last time.*

Avalyn was troubled, though not surprised, to read that Sherman had made a written request for self-termination to the prison physician. He had sent a copy of this letter to the paper, which was published in part within the article Avalyn was reading, "I, Joseph Sherman, being of sound mind, request physician-assisted termination of my life according to state statute. I have been diagnosed with a terminal illness and wish to avoid prolonged suffering."

The article concluded with a statement that Joseph Sherman indeed qualified under the state statute and had publically announced in a written statement through his attorney that today he would proceed with terminating his life.

Avalyn looked at her watch. She had been so consumed with the news that she failed to notice the time. She was on the verge of being late. If she rushed and did not get stuck in traffic, she might avoid another reprimand from her superiors. She pushed away from the table, leaving the remainder of her breakfast untouched.

CHAPTER TWO

AVALYN'S ASSIGNED TASK

"There is no 'they.' He, Mr. Sherman, is going to terminate his own life today. This is his decision. We are only spectators. If he dies today, he will die at his own hands."

-Gloria Wirth, RN
Prison Nursing Supervisor

Avalyn raced out of her neighborhood to join the rush of morning commuters. She squinted over her dash to see through the heavy drops of an early morning rain which partially obscured her view. Several miles of tail lights stretched out ahead of her in the pre-dawn traffic. She looked down to turn on the radio. When she looked up, she gasped. Another car had whipped into her lane and had come to a sudden full stop.

Avalyn grabbed the wheel with both hands and forced her foot onto the brake pedal. She felt the antilock brakes pulsate beneath her foot. The Doppler-enhanced screech of tires and horns came from behind, followed by the unmistakable crush of metal and exploding plastic from cars in the lanes around her. She braced for an impact; none came. Her car was not directly involved in the crash. Seconds passed. She noticed people emerging from various cars, their shadows magnified against a backdrop of exhaust and smoke, illuminated by vehicle headlights. Avalyn thought surely someone had been hurt.

She grabbed a small red medic bag from her center console and ran toward the smoking cars. She donned gloves from her bag and began assessing the scene. One car seemed severely marred. She bent over through a shattered window to speak with an elderly woman sitting in shock behind the wheel; the woman had bright red blood streaming down her forehead as she sat staring blankly forward.

A tall man dressed in rough canvas overalls and leather boots paced behind Avalyn yelling obscenities, "There was no warning! She just stopped right in front of me! Of all the idiotic drivers!"

Avalyn handed her phone to the man. "Take this and dial 911." Instantly calmed by being given a meaningful task, the man took the phone and began dialing. Avalyn turned back to attend the injured driver. She wiped the woman's wounds with gauze from her bag and cracked open an ice bag to place over a swelling knot on the woman's forehead.

Avalyn felt someone tapping on her back. She slid out of the wrecked car; the man handed the phone back to Avalyn, "They want to talk to you."

Avalyn took the call and spoke to emergency services personnel. At one point she climbed atop one of the cars to get a better view of the scene and to direct an ambulance through the traffic jam to the most critical site.

From her vantage point she saw two paramedics dressed in fire resistant turnout pants, the type firefighters wear, running toward her position, weaving their way between cars. Avalyn raised her hand and waved them in the direction of the injured woman. Then she jumped down from the car and ran to help the two men provide emergency care.

Once the woman was safely out of her car, lying supine on a backboard on the pavement, the paramedics worked to secure the elderly woman's stiff, arthritic neck to the backboard.

Avalyn thought, *this woman needs fluid.*

She instinctively grabbed a catheter needle and tourniquet from the paramedics' emergency bag. As she inserted the needle into the woman's arm, Avalyn's hand quivered causing the needle to puncture the side of a blood vessel. A large bruise began to form under the old woman's fragile skin. Avalyn applied pressure and looked up at the paramedics, "I'm sorry, I just blew your vein."

One of the paramedics smiled, "Happens to the best of us, ma'am." Then the paramedic secured a tourniquet to the opposite arm and slid a catheter into a large vein.

Avalyn, self-conscious and not a little ashamed of her failed attempt to be helpful, took a bag of intravenous fluid. She held up the bag and opened the valve to allow lifesaving fluid to flow into the woman's arm.

The other paramedic stood up and patted Avalyn on the back, "You work well under pressure. Ever thought about joining the department?" He couldn't resist the recruiting opportunity for the chronically short-staffed municipal fire department.

Avalyn gave the fireman a smiling wink and answered, "No, thank you. I put out my share of fires every day."

Avalyn returned to her car and tuned her radio to a local station. She listened to the news as traffic began to inch forward. The morning report focused on the planned death of Joseph Sherman. The news reporter added layers to what was already known about his requested "termination of life" as they called it. The termination was scheduled to occur in the prison infirmary under the guidance of prison physicians and prison officials.

Avalyn picked up her phone to call her supervisor, "I'm running late. There was an accident."

"You were in an accident?"

"I'm fine. A lady behind me was hit pretty hard. I stayed to help the paramedics." Even as the words came out she knew it was the wrong thing to say. She braced for the verbal reprimand.

"I don't mean to sound cold, but you are not being paid to serve as a volunteer paramedic. I need you in the infirmary. We are short-staffed, and I can't pay people overtime every time you are late for work."

"I'm sorry ma'am. I really am."

"It's your paycheck," the supervisor said in a clipped tone. "But no matter; everyone is delayed this morning. It's like a circus out front."

"What's going on?"

"The media, protesters, human rights advocates, you name it. It's developing into a sick reality show. The officers have to escort staff through the crowd. Prepare yourself. Somehow it feels like we're the bad guys today."

Avalyn pulled up to the prison entrance gate. A large crowd of people congested the parking entrance shouting rival slogans as if at a sporting event. People in the assembly squinted at Avalyn's oncoming headlights and sluggishly parted to let her vehicle through.

Demonstrators on either side of the road held signs with competing messages partially visible in the early rays of daylight: DEATH is NOT dignified; STOP CAPITAL PUNISHMENT by SUICIDE; ProChoice to the End of Life; Only Jesus had a RIGHT to DIE; and Whatever happened to First Do No Harm? A lady waved her sign in front of Avalyn's windshield and chanted with a small group, "Give me liberty AT my death."

In the midst of angry protesters, Avalyn saw an older lady standing quietly next to a plywood sign. A large picture, displayed on the sign, depicted a striking young lady, smiling and happy. The old woman, by contrast, bore a melancholy expression, her wrinkles turned downward. The woman stood with a hand on the homemade display drawing attention to the sign's somber message: He Killed My Sweet Lyndsay.

Avalyn drove slowly through the crowd; she passed the guard at the gate and found a space in the employee parking area. She could see another crowd beginning to clog the entrance to the prison. Two television trucks with raised satellite antennae blocked her view of the front doors.

Avalyn stepped out of her car and pulled the hood of her jacket over her head, reasoning that people would make way for someone who looked more like a prison visitor. She was wrong.

A reporter in the crowd saw Avalyn's nursing scrub pants and leapt at her with a microphone, "Excuse me, miss, would you answer a few questions?"

Avalyn felt a knot form in her throat. She was brave, but public speaking terrified her. A microphone in her face might as well have been a gun pointed at her mouth. Her heart pounded. She scanned the crowd for an opening, an escape. But her path was blocked ahead, and the mass of people closed in behind her. She felt the suffocating panic of a person who had fallen suddenly into river rapids. She yelled at the reporter over the din, "I have no comment."

"Do you know Joseph Sherman? Can you confirm he is going to die today? How will he do it?"

The reporter's persistence felt like a personal verbal assault to Avalyn, and she instinctively batted the microphone down and held her hand in front of the camera. She later laughed at how this must have made her actually look like a criminal.

As she forced her way forward, a man yelled, "Let the killers go do their work." This struck a negative chord in Avalyn. Offended, she turned and raised a finger in the man's face, "How dare you suggest…."

Before she could complete the phrase an attentive officer slid behind her and grabbed her by the shoulders. He called out, "Good morning, Nurse Robbins. Come with me." He swung her around and guided her through the crowd to the entryway where he used a key card to open a side entrance door.

Once inside, Avalyn walked through the first of two security check points. The first looked like security at an airport where passengers remove shoes and place bags on a belt for scanning, and individuals walk through a metal detector.

An officer saw Avalyn and waved her through the first check point. She walked through the crowded waiting area toward the employee sally port. A few people looked up from seats along the perimeter of the room and watched her pass.

The room was already crowded with family members of inmates, clergy, and attorneys impatiently waiting to see inmates for scheduled contact time. These people had trickled in early to get a preferred spot on the visitors' schedule.

As Avalyn passed through the waiting room, she was momentarily distracted by a tired mother with weathered hair and bright lipstick, holding a baby. No doubt they had come to see one of the prisoners. A toddler was standing at the woman's side pulling at her arm. Avalyn overheard the little boy ask, "When's Daddy wakin' up, Mommy?"

Avalyn thought of home. Her children would soon be pulling the covers off the bed of their daddy. She imagined their voices, giggling, "Wake up, Daddy."

The loud unmistakable bang of a magnetic lock broke her daydream. "Nurse Robbins, are you coming through?" An officer stood beside the door holding it open. He motioned for Avalyn to enter with a few other people.

Avalyn entered the sally port with several officers, an attorney, and a fellow nurse.

"Time to board the morning bus," said one of the officers.

"Bus?" asked the attorney.

Avalyn looked over at the sharply dressed attorney who had stooped to lower a file box he was carrying. She whispered lowly, "Kind of feels like getting on a crowded bus, don't you think?"

A voice over the intercom asked mechanically,

"What's in the box, sir?"

The attorney appeared startled. He looked toward an overhead speaker as if speaking to an unseen higher power, "Just files to review with my client."

"Open the box, please."

The attorney removed the lid revealing a row of file folders stuffed with paperwork. An officer standing next to him saw one of the labeled files on top and said, "Sherman, huh? Looks like a high profile case for you today."

"So much for attorney-client privileges," quipped the attorney.

"Sorry, couldn't resist."

In the prison, the sally port functions as a two-way safety valve for people entering or leaving the facility. Each port is built like an airlock with a door on each end of an extended room. Only one door can be opened at a time. This effectively traps the occupants in security's version of purgatory, a resting place or a torturous pause between the land of the free and the world of the prisoner. A large one-way mirror along one wall of the port allows control officers on the other side of the window to verify each person's identity and visually inspect items brought into the facility.

A cold, mechanized voice came over the intercom, "Place your I.D. and keys in the tray."

Each person placed a set of car keys and a form of identification into a tray slot under the mirrored window. The slot reopened with a collection of employee key cards and one card labeled PROFESSIONAL VISITOR.

Avalyn grabbed the badge bearing her name and photo. She clipped it to her shirt. The second door opened with a buzz and a bang.

Avalyn made her way down a wide corridor with bland green walls and a polished floor. She felt a nervous pressure to get to her post quickly. She looked at her watch. *I'm so late*, she thought. She broke into a near-jog, stopping in front of a door marked MEDICAL. Avalyn waved her badge over a key card reader on the wall. She passed quickly through the busy medical department, breathlessly saying good morning to colleagues. On the far side of the clinic was a door into the infirmary, a segregated medical wing. Avalyn swiped her card at this door and ran into the infirmary. Here she came face to face with her supervisor, who sat impatiently at the nurses' desk.

The nurses' desk, a solid metal work space salvaged from a World War II era office complex, was positioned centrally behind a low concrete counter in the center of a large, circular room lined with individual treatment cells. The infirmary looked like an ICU in many respects. Glass-doored treatment rooms opened into the central work area. A medication cart and a separate supply cart stood next to the nurses' station. Inmates in various stages of treatment waited out the hours, some sitting in bedside wheelchairs, others reclined in hospital beds, many of them hooked to IV tubes and some breathing through oxygen cannulas. If one were to close his or her eyes and just listen, the sounds in the infirmary would be identical to a hospital ward with beeping machines and monitors.

But the infirmary was no ordinary medical ward. The cells were designed for the treatment of prisoners, some very dangerous, who despite losing many rights as citizens, did not lose a fundamental right to essential health care. Even killers grow old, get sick, and need medical care. The infirmary was the prisoners' equivalent of a skilled nursing facility. For some it was a temporary stop for rehabilitation; for others it was a final home.

In a prison infirmary, public safety and human rights are held in balanced tension. Most people in the free world would wisely avoid close contact with violent criminals, but health care intrinsically requires some level of human contact. Nearly everything a nurse does for a patient requires close proximity.

But Avalyn and her fellow nurses rarely spoke of fear in their unique workplace. Every corner of the prison environment was on camera. Officers, sometimes in pairs, stood abreast the medical staff at each patient encounter. Patients in orange prison garb received their treatments behind shatter-proof glass doors. Avalyn often told concerned friends that she felt safer at work than she did at the mall.

The medical staff counted every medical item and every piece of equipment daily. Even the smallest article could be misused as a weapon or sold as contraband. Staples, tape, tubing, alcohol swabs, scissors, needles, bandages, and braces were inventoried daily to prevent theft or diversion. Medical staff members learned to maintain a defensive stance when assessing a patient and to be cautious when leaning in close to listen with a stethoscope or to change a bandage.

Avalyn rushed up to her supervisor, a woman named Gloria Wirth. Gloria was stocky, not so much obese but large and athletic in frame. She had the gravelly voice of a chain smoker and wiry blond hair that appeared to have been washed in solvent to remove the smell of tobacco. She had perpetually good posture which seemed to reflect an inner confidence. She earned her position by keeping problems off the desk of her superiors. A master at effectively managing people, her nurses both feared and loved her. She displayed few emotions, at least none that were seen by others, her affect was perpetually flat, neither smiling nor frowning. She rarely revealed the feeling behind her directives. Yet she made herself understood, and more than that, she had the intimidating ability to make people bend to her will. Even inmates stood up straighter when she walked by.

Avalyn was partially out of breath having run from the sally port to the medical wing. She bent over the desk to speak with her supervisor, "Gloria, I'm so sorry to make you wait."

The supervisor lowered her reading glasses to the desk, "I think you will earn your pay today. Sit down. I need to brief you on the panel of patients."

Avalyn caught the unusually ominous tone in Gloria's voice. She wiped the sweat from her forehead as she sat down and then pulled a pen from her pocket to record details.

Most of her patients would have routine needs like

post-operative orders, pre-operative preparations, and treatment orders.

The supervisor opened Sherman's chart on the computer screen. "Are you familiar with Joseph Sherman?"

"Too familiar. He's all over the news this morning."

"Let me show you why. Here is the doctor's order."

Avalyn scanned the doctor's orders. She read the final line aloud in a hushed tone. "Secobarbital nine thousand milligrams by mouth. Keep on person." She turned to her supervisor, "When was the order written?"

"Two weeks ago. The order becomes active today. Doctor Brant will be by soon for rounds. Please make sure he confirms the order with the pharmacy. They must have a wet-signed original script before ten this morning to fill the order."

Avalyn thought back to her first encounters with Sherman. At one point she remembered that Sherman had submitted an application for a medical parole and outside hospice care. The closing lines from his application stood out to her as being memorable if not cryptically poetic, "My body now serves a sentence for crimes of which my soul is no longer guilty."

Avalyn looked at Gloria, "What about his application for parole?"

Gloria clicked a tab on the screen and scrolled through a document, "It looks like his application was reviewed by the board over a month ago. He was denied."

"So they are just going to let him do it? Just let him take the pills and die? What are they thinking?"

"There is no 'they.' He, Mr. Sherman, is going to terminate his own life today. This is his decision. We are only spectators. If he dies today, he will die at his own hands."

"I understand. But who will give him the meds?" Avalyn looked puzzled.

Her supervisor maintained a silent gaze.

"The pharmacist?"

"No, Avalyn."

"Doctor Brant?"

"Humph. That's wishful thinking."

"Are you saying I have to give him the pills?"

"Avalyn. You are on shift today. Your job is to dispense medications as prescribed. The form of the medication does not change your job."

"What if I refuse?"

"It is well within your right to refuse. Just make sure you have a well-reasoned rationale. And be prepared to submit it in writing. Human resources considers baseless refusal to perform duties as grounds for dismissal."

Avalyn felt the weight of professional coercion. She responded sluggishly, as if trying to summon specific words from a partially-learned foreign language, words that she herself had never articulated, "Surely nurses are not expected to hand out lethal doses of medication."

Gloria turned to face Avalyn. She said, "Sometimes taking the high road means taking a hard road. I know you'll do the right thing."

Avalyn looked up to see her supervisor turn her back and walk away, speaking some command over her radio which prompted the door to buzz open at the edge of the infirmary.

Avalyn watched her boss leave. She felt a growing sense of abandonment; her head fell forward into her hands, *Can I really do this?*

Avalyn suddenly felt very alone.

CHAPTER THREE

MORNING ROUNDS IN THE INFIRMARY

"In my work, I get to meet crazy people when they are sober and in their right minds. The rest of the world sees the convict at his worst; I may be one of the few people who gets to see the real person, preferably at his best."

- Avalyn Robbins, RN
Prison Nurse

But Avalyn was not alone. A warm, deep voice with a Caribbean accent called her name, "You feelin' well, Nurse Robbins?"

Avalyn turned to see an officer standing at the officers' desk. He was short, with broad shoulders and a protuberant belly. His dark black skin matched his deep brown eyes. "Good morning, Officer Vatel. I am fine, thank you."

Vatel had overheard the conversation. He offered a strange consolation, "There may be mountains beyond the mountains, Nurse Robbins, but we'll get you there; you'll see."

Avalyn had no idea what that meant. But she knew Vatel well enough to know he meant to give her a boost. Vatel handed out words and proverbs like gifts.

Frantz Vatel was a naturalized citizen. He grew up in Haiti as an orphan. On his fourteenth birthday, he was adopted by a missionary couple and brought to the United States. Even after years of living in the States, he had never lost the island accent or his love for Haitian proverbs.

A fellow Haitian who knew Vatel in the orphanage once wrote a biography of Vatel entitled *The Little Protector*, in which Vatel was described as boy who stood watch over younger orphans at a children's home in Northern Haiti. Chapter one described him fighting off larger, older bullies who tried to steal food from the younger children. Another chapter described a clandestine trip Vatel took back to the orphanage when he was twenty-one, after one of Haiti's political uprisings; he crossed secretly into Haiti by first flying to the Dominican Republic and then crossing the northern border by boat at night. He risked his life to deliver supplies and money to children who, living as Vatel once lived, struggled to survive without parents in a forgotten corner of the world. The book ended with a touching description of a badge ceremony where one of those young orphans was invited to the United States to pin the badge on Officer Vatel's uniform upon his graduation from the Officer Training Academy.

Avalyn gathered her instruments and unlocked the wheels of the medication cart. She gave Vatel a worried grin, "We have a lot to do in a short time. You ready to see patients?"

"Yes ma'am. I got your back, Nurse Robbins. These men are fortunate to have you as their nurse. Don't you worry. I'll make them behave."

The prison infirmary was made up of standard prison cells specially adapted for medical treatment. Here inmates received the highest level of health care offered in a prison facility. The unit was usually full.

Avalyn began with a brief check on each of the inmate-patients. She pushed the medication cart to the door of room one and looked at information on a computer tablet secured atop the cart. Without looking up, she spoke to Vatel, "We need to move quickly this morning. Doctor Brant will be here to round in less than an hour. The good doctor is an impatient man." She paused to click a field on the computer. Then she looked up at Vatel as if to emphasize her point and whispered, "My husband says Doctor Brant is so high strung he makes meth look sedating."

"Impatience is the façade of insecurity, ma'am. If I may say, when you work with the doctor, you strike me as a very patient person."

"Thank you, Vatel. But let's not worsen the good doctor's insecurity this morning. Would you open cell one for me?"

Vatel looked through the shatter-proof window to see the inmate in cell one asleep on a hospital-type bed. His left leg was elevated, and an IV was dripping into his left arm. He had wrapped a homemade blindfold over his eyes, a common practice among inmates who design functional sleeping masks by tucking each toe of a pair of socks into the open side of the alternate sock so as to form a soft loop which they place over their eyes to block overhead lights. Vatel took a large bronze-colored key from his belt and opened the door. He walked over to the bed and pulled the sock mask up off the inmate's eyes.

"Wake up, Mr. Cunningham. The nurse is here to see you."

The inmate squinted under the bright fluorescent lights and wiped his eyes. He took a deep, audible breath and spoke in a patronizing manner, "Good morning.

How is Avalyn this morning?"

Avalyn stood erect, taking on the commanding demeanor of a drill sergeant, "Mr. Cunningham, you are still in prison where we will address each other formally. I am to be called Nurse Robbins. Is that understood?" She was not being unkind or overly formal. Inmates are known for manipulating staff. And almost every attempt at manipulation begins with an inmate's calling a person by his or her first name. Familiarity breeds disarming trust.

Mr. Cunningham responded to Avalyn's reprimand with a stern piercing stare, his nose uplifted like a guard dog sniffing for any traces of fear or deceit; but finding her to be equally stern, serious in both tone and stance, Mr. Cunningham withdrew his gaze and extended his arm for a blood pressure check as a gesture of submission.

Avalyn moved efficiently. She took Mr. Cunningham's blood pressure and temperature. She hung a new bag of medication and pulled back the sheet to expose a red, swollen leg, "Hmm. The infection is not spreading, but it's certainly not looking better. Something is not right; you've been on the antibiotic for several days. I should think it would have improved by now. I'll ask the Doc to see you today."

Mr. Cunningham recognized the encounter was quickly coming to a close. He noted Avalyn's hurried manner and thought this an opportunity to get something extra; sometimes saying yes is just easier when people are pressed for time. So he raised a standard barrage of predictable questions formulated to boost the ego and soften the defenses of the medical staff, "I know you care and are very busy and can see I'm in pain. Would you ask the doctor about increasing my pain medication? I don't want to get hooked on anything. I don't even like the stuff. I just need something a little stronger until the antibiotics start working, you see. And could you ask the kitchen to send me a double portion at dinner or at least an evening snack? I remember the doctor saying I need extra protein to boost my immune system. And one more thing; my eye doctor prescribed tinted glasses for my scintillations and light-sensitivities. You are very smart, so I know you know what that means and these lights are just in my eyes all day because I'm on my back. Would you have any influence over the property officer to explain why I need the dark glasses for medical reasons?...."

The questions did not stop, and would not stop, until Avalyn politely answered in a firm, almost rehearsed manner with the same response she gave every inmate who had ever raised the same list of tiresome questions, "The doctor will be here soon. You may ask him."

"Very well. Thank you and God bless." Mr. Cunningham leaned back and pulled the socks back over his eyes.

Avalyn and Vatel repeated a similar routine in each room. Like musicians making their way from table to table around a fine restaurant Avalyn and Vatel made their way to each cell.

The inmate in room two was fasting in preparation for a colonoscopy. He was sitting up in the hospital-style bed drinking from a clear plastic cup. A partially consumed jug of some cathartic mixture sat on his bedside table.

Avalyn caught his attention through the cell's large window. She yelled through the crack in the door, "Drink up, Mr. Gianni. The transport officers will be by this morning to get you."

Mr. Gianni raised his cup toward the window. He face fell into a sour grimace to indicate his opinion of the flavor as he sarcastically yelled back, "Cheers!"

The inmate in room three was under observation for head trauma. He had returned from the hospital the previous night after repair of a blowout fracture of his right orbit sustained in a prison altercation. Calling the fight an altercation was a euphemistic way of deflecting attention away from the true mechanism of injury. Officers who witnessed the attack said it was a premeditated execution of prison justice. The inmate had been convicted of sexually assaulting young boys at a camp. Word of his behavior spread quickly throughout the prison, and once the verdict became public knowledge within the general prison population, the injured inmate had become a target. Even criminally-minded felons have worked out an internal system of justice, one that restores a Levitical code of taking an eye for an eye and a tooth for a tooth. When it comes to meting out due punishment, according to the prisoners' code, crimes against children are near capital offenses. The inmate in cell three was lucky to be alive.

The inmate in cell four was suffering from an alcohol-induced encephalopathy whereby withdrawal from alcohol induced an abrupt reawakening of his brain after months of stupor. He could no longer separate reality from dreams; gremlins populated his cell; visitors entered and exited through a mirror above the sink; he became paranoid of any real human being and saw personal threat in every piece of medical equipment. For most of the day he sat huddled in a fetal position at the head of his bed.

Avalyn greeted the inmate cautiously, "Good morning, Mr. Thomas."

As soon as he heard his name, his head whipped toward the door. He acknowledged the presence of the nurse and officer with a silent, demonic stare. In a few seconds, he began shaking like a man consumed with anger and yelled, "You cannot have me! I will not die! I will not let you do it! Heeeelp meee!"

Mr. Thomas perceived something far different than what was real. He was listening to an old drinking buddy, long deceased, telling him to come with him through the mirror into the depths of Hades. He saw Avalyn walk through the door, not with a stethoscope, but with a venomous snake around her neck. She was approaching Mr. Thomas, holding the head of the snake with fangs protruding; presumably she was attempting to assassinate Mr. Thomas with the venom. Vatel was a large black soldier perceived by Mr. Thomas to be an enforcer of the entire plot against him.

Of course nothing of this dream was true. But the delirious inability of the patient to distinguish between the genuine and the delusion made him unpredictable, explosive even.

Mr. Thomas lunged at Avalyn, his eyes fixed on her stethoscope, as he grasped wildly at what he perceived to be a venomous threat. In the struggle he was able to rip the stethoscope away from Avalyn. He grasped the stethoscope with both hands, swung it over his head erratically, and smashed it repeatedly against the floor.

Avalyn felt the sudden burn of the stethoscope tubing being ripped from her neck. Though startled, she maintained a professional calm. She lifted a stiff arm against the patient's advances and defensively stepped backward out of the room calling instructions to Vatel, "Get him to the bed. He's confused."

Vatel could not have known what nightmare possessed the inmate; he could only see the inmate's anger was focused on the stethoscope. In one defensive move, Vatel stepped in front of the inmate and wrestled the swinging stethoscope from his hands. "Be calm, Mr. Thomas; you are safe. Nurse Robbins is here to help you. See, we are taking the bad thing away."

Having disarmed the delusional inmate, Vatel tossed the bent stethoscope back to Avalyn and used his radio to call in the help of a roving officer.

Avalyn stepped outside the cell. With surprisingly calm hands she prepared an injectable sedative. She squirted a few drops from an upraised syringe and called out, "I'm ready when you are, Officer."

Vatel's training enabled him to maneuver the inmate into a face-down posture on the bed. With the help of a fellow officer, he restrained the inmate in this prone position, an action to which the inmate objected with increasing vehemence; but the restraint afforded protection to both the patient and the provider, allowing Avalyn to safely administer an injection into Mr. Thomas' exposed buttocks.

The shot was predictably perceived as the bite of a viper. So for several minutes the inmate screamed obscenities and begged for his life, but once the medication took effect, he curled back into a fetal position on the bed and drifted off to sleep.

The sounds of erratic screaming about a snake loose in a patient's cell did nothing for the therapeutic environment of the infirmary.

Inmates from other cells started banging shoes against the windows and yelling from the cracks in their cell doors, "Nurse…Nurse…nuuuuurse."

Avalyn ignored the pandemonium and followed Vatel to the next cell.

Vatel placed a key into the lock of the door to cell five. He looked back at Avalyn, "Looks like we've got a mess to clean up. Mr. Fernando is quite the Poocasso this morning ."

It is not uncommon for an inmate to protest incarceration by smearing feces over the walls of his cell, prompting the moniker "Poocasso."

Fernando stood behind the door, naked and disheveled, with feces smeared over himself and the walls of his cell. The smell of human waste seeped under the cell door.

"Sit down on your bunk, Fernando," ordered Vatel,

his voice booming loudly so as to be heard through the glass window of the cell door.

Fernando shook his head wildly, "I will not move until I see him."

"You must sit down, Fernando. I cannot open your cell until you are seated."

Fernando again protested, "I will not move from this spot. You cannot stop him."

"Who? Who do you wish to see Fernando?"

Fernando pounded his fist on the glass in pure anger. Then he pointed a threatening finger at Vatel, "I will not talk to you. I want to see Jesus Christ. I want to see him now."

Avalyn heard the inmate's request. She felt annoyed and pressed for time. She rolled her eyes sarcastically, "I really don't have time for this. I'm calling the expert."

Avalyn walked to the nurses' station. She picked up a phone and dialed the office of the prison chaplain.

Chaplain Moffat arrived quickly. He was an eighty-year-old man, tall in stature, with a large, slightly hunched frame and partially atrophied musculature. His slick white hair was brushed straight back, giving him the appearance of being in perpetual forward motion. And he did move, briskly with very little rest, hampered only by a slight limp from an old hip injury. He wore a nicely tailored sports jacket, no tie, and running shoes, which did not seem out of place for him. The only feature besides his hair that clearly belied his age was an old pair of reading glasses which he wore continually on the tip of his nose. The Chaplain had worked in the prison for over thirty years.

When someone asked when he was going to retire he would smile and say, "Retirement is for old people." He was known for speaking the truth even when the truth hurt, and for this he was well respected by inmates and staff alike. He had a way of tending his flock of black sheep as a loving shepherd. "I'm not a hug-a-thug," he would say, "but every person deserves to know they matter to at least one other human being on this planet."

Avalyn had come to appreciate the chaplain's approach to addressing the spiritual stresses of prison life. He took all religions seriously, "All truth is God's truth," he would say. But he was not afraid of pointing out where a person's belief crossed a line and became a potential source of moral impairment, or worse, a delusion.

Chaplain Moffat walked up to cell number five. He looked at the naked, unruly man on the opposite side of the glass and asked, "Fernando, my friend, you are a mess. What is the problem?"

Fernando repeated his demand, "I want to see Jesus, and I want to see him now!"

Chaplain Moffat smiled warmly and calmly tapped at his watch, "Fernando, the Bible says no one knows the hour or day of his coming, not even angels, but I can tell you that visiting hours do not start until eight. You know that. Jesus will have to wait until eight, just like everyone else. You should let the nurse clean you up so when He comes you are ready."

Fernando furrowed his brow and looked downward. After a moment he looked back at the Chaplain, "Will you wash me?"

Chaplain Moffat could clearly see the walls and the inmate smeared in filth. The smell of feces emanating from around the cell door filled his nostrils. But if the scene or smell bothered him, it did not show. He simply looked warmly into the eyes of the inmate. Then he smiled, a big child-like smile, as if he suddenly recognized an old friend. "It would be my honor."

Fernando shrugged his bare shoulders and walked back to sit on his bunk.

Avalyn looked at the Chaplain, "How did you do that?"

Vatel opened the door. The nauseating smell of feces rolled out of the room. Chaplain Moffat took a rag, moistened it in the cell sink and gently wiped feces from Fernando's hands, feet, and body.

This gave Avalyn an opportunity to check Fernando's vital signs and give him his morning medications.

Outside the cell, Avalyn expressed her appreciation to the chaplain, "Thank you for your help. I know that was not how you wanted to spend your morning."

"On the contrary, my dear, that is exactly how I wanted to spend my morning."

Avalyn gave the chaplain a strange, suspicious look, "You are kidding. Right?"

The Chaplain leaned forward and lowered his voice, "It is no chore for an old preacher to wash the feet of a hungry, thirsty, naked stranger who happens to be sick and in prison. For me it is the highest honor."

The chaplain turned to the sink. As he washed his hands, he asked, "How is Mr. Sherman today?"

Avalyn leaned toward the chaplain and whispered, "Did you know he plans to…um…take his own life…today?"

The chaplain winked and whispered, "I've known Mr. Sherman a long time; I believe he's prepared for the day of his passing. But I'll swing by to visit with him in a few hours. Maybe he will let this old man in on the new secret."

Chaplain Moffat laughed as he turned to exit the infirmary as briskly as he had arrived.

Avalyn returned to her rounds. She introduced herself to a newly remanded prisoner in cell number six, an inmate with the last name Zachary, admitted to the infirmary for an acute paralysis sustained after he was restrained by officers for fighting with another inmate during the intake process. "Mr. Zachary, I am Nurse Robbins. I will be taking care of you today. Do you have any concerns for the doctor?"

Mr. Zachary sat on the edge of his bed using only his left arm to move into position. His right arm hung limply at his side. He met Avalyn with angry words, "You see this? I was physically assaulted at your facility by your officers. What kind of operation is this? They handcuffed me behind my back for hours and left me alone in a cold cell just to piss all over myself. You ever try to take a piss with your hands tied behind you? Now I'm in pain and my arm is paralyzed. My hand is paralyzed from the cuffs. I can't move my arm. The officer sat full force with his knee on my back. He is so sued. It hurts all the way into my hand. I cannot sleep. I am suffering. Look at my hand. I cannot even pick up a spoon to eat. And now you prance in here and ask if I have any concerns? I hope you have good lawyers."

Avalyn listened patiently to the inappropriate rant. It would be a mistake, however, to assume she was listening passively; in reality she was watching every movement for objective signs of pain or dysfunction. A person can easily lie with words, but it is very hard to lie with the whole body. "May I examine your hand?" Avalyn asked.

"Whatever it takes, lady. But I'm telling you, it hurts."

Avalyn performed a brief, well-rehearsed screening exam designed to test for real weakness or pain while diverting the patient's attention toward something else. She spoke professionally but constantly, like a magician using patter to keep her audience distracted from what she was really doing. Real pain and real weakness persist even with distraction. Mr. Zachary's symptoms did not persist with distraction. She lightly touched the inmate's right hand, to which he screamed out in pain. Then she grabbed his opposite shoulder and asked if the shoulder hurt, while she was actually squeezing the supposedly painful right hand again, but this time he made no complaint of hand pain. Then when she returned to focus on the right hand, the symptoms reappeared.

"See, Nurse? It's like I had a stroke or something. I'm telling you, it hurts."

Avalyn did not react. She did not smile. She did not frown. She did not explain how a stroke does not usually cause pain. She did not explain how his complaints were inconsistent with his exam. She did not accuse him of faking. She just turned to walk away.

"What are you going to give me for the pain?" the inmate yelled.

Avalyn replied, "Nothing, Mr. Zachary. Your exam is inconsistent with your complaints. I will let the doctor decide whether or not you should get medication for pain."

The inmate heard the reply. He knew he had been tricked. His face tensed in raw anger. Without thinking he reflexively raised his right hand to make an obscene gesture at Avalyn.

Avalyn looked at Mr. Zachary's belligerent right-handed gesture. *Some people make it way too easy*, she thought. She shook her head while raising her shoulders and hands in a what-can-I-say motion. She turned to Vatel and said, "Officer, please report Mr. Zachary's behavior to the disciplinary board; they will be reassured to know that his paralysis has resolved."

Avalyn next entered cell seven. The inmate sitting in a bedside chair looked up from reading a book. His glance initially gave Avalyn cold chills. It was like looking death in the eyes. The inmate's name was Rico Velasquez, a thirty-year-old man with a bald head and a body decorated with tattoos. His body was a pure work of art, a living canvas on which a master tattoo artist had left his masterpiece. The right side of Mr. Velasquez, from the tip of his head to the soles of his feet, was tattooed with layered images depicting the bones and organs that lay beneath the skin. At first glance, it appeared as though his skin had been ripped from one half of his body with the underlying tissue remaining vibrant and exposed. The right side of his face was a perfect representation of a skull with even the whites of his right eye tattooed black to give the appearance of an empty eye socket.

Avalyn forced herself to look at the inmate without following her instinct to look away, "Good morning, Mr. Velasquez. How is the hip?"

Rico lifted himself to an unsteady standing position. His reluctance to put full weight on his right hip seemed to accentuate the artwork on this half of his body, as though he truly felt pain on the virtually exposed side. Once standing on both feet he pointed to his right hip and smiled, "Look at this. I'm a new man. The Doc says I got titanium in there. I'm able to stand under my own power. What do you think?"

Avalyn smiled, "I think you're going to need a revision of your tattoo to show the artificial hip."

"Do you think I could be cleared to return to general population?"

"We will see what Doc Brant has to say."

"Sounds good," Velasquez responded while lowering himself back to the chair.

Avalyn closed the cell door and suddenly heard the inmate in the next cell singing. Something about the resonant effects of cinderblock gives people the false perception of musical talent. But like a person singing in the shower or singing with headphones, the only one who usually enjoys the performance is the singer himself.

The inmate stopped singing as soon as he heard the key rotate in his cell door. Avalyn entered the cell and wrapped a blood pressure cuff around the inmate's arm. She looked at the reading on the machine and shook her head. This cannot be correct, she thought.

The inmate saw the concerned look in her eyes, "Is it bad, nurse? Is it still high?"

"Are you having any problems with headaches or visual changes?"

"No ma'am. I feel pretty good."

"Well your blood pressure remains dangerously high. I can't explain it. Most people respond well to the medication."

"That's what they always say."

"Always?"

"The doctors say it's just my response to you medical people."

"White coat hypertension?"

"Maybe. But you ain't wearin' no coat."

"It doesn't matter. I have an idea. Do you like to sing?"

"Well I like to sing in here. It's like being inside your very own subwoofer."

"Ok then, let's try something. You keep singing. And let me check your blood pressure again."

As the inmate began his singing, which Avalyn later described as sounding more like wailing, she ran the blood pressure machine through a cycle. Then Avalyn turned the machine so the inmate could see the numbers. "See, your blood pressure is more normal."

"What does that mean? I thought you said it was still bad?"

"I think you have an overly sensitive autonomic nervous system. I bet people say you're hot-tempered. Singing seems to settle it down nicely. Here, take your medication. It seems to be working fine. I'll inform Doctor Brant that your hypertension appears to be well controlled; maybe he will lower your dosage." Avalyn handed two pills to the inmate and walked out.

A neighbor once asked Avalyn if she felt scared taking care of murderers, drug addicts, thieves, and sex offenders. She replied, "In my work, I get to meet crazy people when they are sober and in their right minds. The rest of the world sees the convict at his worst; I may be one of the few people who gets to see the real person, preferably at his best." Then she added, "Sometimes the real person is an amazing individual."

The inmate in the next cell was a good example. His name was Justin Matthews, a civil engineer by training, serving time because of a dependence on cocaine, which not only ruined his family and career, but also caused his heart to age at an accelerated rate. He was recovering from open heart surgery. He was sitting at a metallic desk on a metal stool, both of which were bolted to the floor. He was meticulously piecing together a small machine of some sort. It appeared to be made entirely out of strips of paper and tape. A bar of soap carved into the shape of a small clock face hung from the machine on a thin string. Avalyn asked him to explain it to her.

"The apparatus is a classic time piece," said Matthews, "similar to the old pendulum clocks. Look here. The string from which the weight is suspended can be wound around this axle made from a pencil shaft. As gravity pulls the soap downward, it causes this paper pendulum to swing between these two paper posts, similar to clicking off seconds."

"Amazing. But does it really tell you the time?"

"Well it's no atomic clock, I can assure you, but it's not bad. You see, it takes two hours for the soap to fall the width of one block on the wall. It's accurate to within about ten minutes and has to be reset every twelve hours. I just pick some known time, such as shift change, and keep time from that point forward. It keeps me sane, you see. There are no windows in here. I think I would become psychotic if I could not keep track of time."

Avalyn stopped outside the next cell. She reached into a drawer on the cart and lifted out a small medication bottle. She poured two pills from the bottle into a small paper medicine cup. Then she took a small pestle and crushed the pills into a powder. She looked over at Vatel and spoke softly, "I may need your help in here."

"I still got your back, Nurse Robbins."

Avalyn entered the cell. She held out the medication cup to the inmate, a lean, suntanned man with a thin nose and large black eyebrows. He wore a long-arm cast, held tightly to his side. He was standing when Avalyn entered his room. Avalyn said, "Good morning Mr. Ostrom. Here is your pain medicine."

"I am supposed to be getting hydrocodone."

"That is hydrocodone."

"So why's it crushed? That's nasty."

"It's prison policy, Mr. Ostrom. Too many people

cheek the medication and sell it."

"Are you accusing me of cheekin' meds? I never sold any of my drugs you guys gave me. You can't punish me for what other people done. You probably took the hydros yourself and are just giving me some generic junk."

Indifferent to the insult, Avalyn held out the medication cup and reiterated, "Are you accusing me of not knowing my job? You can take the medication or not; it does not matter to me. But this is a narcotic, if you want this medication, you will have to take it in a crushed form."

Ostrom grabbed the cup and tossed the powder into his mouth. The bitter dry powder coated his mouth and throat. He grimaced and reached for a cup of water. He took a single gulp and slammed the cup down.

Avalyn stood before him calmly for a moment and then said, "Open your mouth."

"Why? What's your problem?"

Avalyn crossed her arms in a formidable gesture of power, "Swallow checks are required. Show me your mouth."

Ostrom took a step toward her, at first with a threatening pose, but then his demeanor and posture suddenly softened. Vatel had taken a large step to be at Avalyn's side, which nonverbally put Ostrom on notice that he was expected to comply. Failure to do so would result in punitive action.

The inmate opened his mouth. His tongue and throat appeared clear of the medication.

Avalyn remained straight-faced, "Lower your lip please."

Ostrom looked at Vatel, "This woman is impossible. She's harassin' me for no reason. I took the medication. What's her problem? I swallowed it. I showed her my mouth. Now leave me alone!"

Vatel spoke firmly, "You know the rule Ostrom. You treat Nurse Robbins with respect and do as you are told."

The inmate reached up and lowered his lip. A compacted paste of white powder remained in the crevasse between his lower lip and the gum line.

Avalyn immediately walked out of the cell followed by Vatel. As the cell door closed Avalyn said to the inmate, "Mr. Ostrom, you know the policy. Your cheeking will be reported. That is your last dose of the narcotic."

The inmate responded with a predictable outburst of anger, hurling verbal insults and obscenities at Avalyn and Officer Vatel. But Avalyn's actions were fully justified. Ostrom had previously stood before the disciplinary board twice for diverting his medications, usually narcotics or antidepressants that could be snorted. In one case, he pretended to swallow his medication and then passed it to others; on another occasion, he made himself vomit to retrieve capsules that he subsequently sold to other inmates.

Avalyn walked into the next cell to find an elderly inmate standing over sorted piles of paperwork neatly organized on his bed. His right hand shook with a pill-rolling tremor which strangely disappeared as he reached to place a form on the bed; the shaking resumed when the hand came again to a resting position. He heard the door open and turned slowly toward Avalyn with a rigid pause between movements as if his body remained slightly out of sync with what his brain was ready to do.

Avalyn extended a cup with several pills, "Here's your meds, Mr. Casselbach."

"Thank you, Nurse Robbins. Say, I'm working on an appeal to get out on medical parole, and I need an expert to verify my condition. May I use you as a witness? You know my condition better than anyone, and it's only a formality, really. I just need you to sign an affidavit for me."

Avalyn held up her hand, "Mr. Casselbach, I am your nurse, not your lawyer. You have every right to argue your case, but I cannot and will not advocate for you in legal matters. Let me stick to the medicine. When it comes to nursing care, you get my best. You'll have to get someone else to help you with the application. Would you like me to make an appointment for you with the medical social worker? She may be able to help you."

"I understand. Thank you, a visit with the social worker would be very kind."

Avalyn walked out and pushed the medication cart up to the door of cell twelve. Beside the cell door was a white board with the inmate's name written in bold, black dry-erase marker, JOSEPH SHERMAN.

Avalyn could feel a nervous tightness in her abdomen. Sherman was planning to terminate his life, possibly that very day. The time had not been set.

Perhaps it would happen in the afternoon, better yet after her shift. Would he request a final meal? Avalyn's mind raced with all the possible questions he might ask when she entered the room. She had no answers. She felt as inexperienced as her first day as a nursing student. She was well trained to provide care to a dying patient. She had sat with many dying patients; her fear was not a fear of death. She simply could not picture herself being the efficient cause of another human's death.

She took a deep breath and opened the cart drawer to locate Mr. Sherman's medications. She noticed her hand shaking as she placed pills in a medication cup atop the cart. She reminded herself that these were only analgesic pills, simple acetaminophen, available over-the-counter, and a few pills for other minor ailments. She was not administering a deadly medication, not yet anyway. She was preparing a medication intended to provide a little relief, nothing more. *But the difference between curing and killing is only a matter of dosage*, she said to herself. This passing thought seemed to creep down Avalyn's spine in a chilling wave of dread.

Vatel watched Avalyn prepare the medication, but he remained silent, standing ready with keys to open the cell door.

The silence was interrupted by a radio call. Vatel's handset sounded a loud pulsating beep, followed by an emergency announcement, "Code blue. Man down, cell block Bravo...code blue. Man down, cell block Bravo...all medical and roving security respond."

Avalyn dropped the pills back onto the cart. She

turned and ran toward the nurses' station, reaching the desk before the second alarm beep ended. She extended her arm under the desk and grabbed at a large red bag. Then she ran for the exit with the bag strap hoisted over her shoulder. As she ran she yelled back, "Confirm Bravo mod?"

"Yes ma'am. Bravo," shouted Vatel as he watched her run out of the infirmary.

CHAPTER FOUR

SUICIDE, FISHING, AND A PROMISE

"Mr. Sherman, you will be treated with compassion and dignity, just like everyone else."

- Avalyn Robbins, RN
Prison Nurse

Avalyn ran up the broad prison stairs. Her heart pounded in anticipation of the emergency awaiting her. Algorithms of life-saving maneuvers flashed through her mind as she prepared for the worst. Was it a cardiac arrest? Did someone try to kill himself? Was there a fight? Would there be one victim or many? She caught up with a fellow nurse and two officers in front of the entry port into the cell block. The officers' radios blared in unison, "Central control, open Bravo doors for medical."

The doors in front of Avalyn and the officers buzzed open. Together, they ran into the cell block and followed the directions of other officers pointing toward the sound of yelling inmates, "Over here! Over here! He's blue! He ain't breathin'!"

The prison cells in Bravo, also called Module B, where built on two square tiers around a large concrete-floored central multipurpose area with rows of heavy plastic chairs facing a wall-mounted television and a number of tables bolted to the floor around which inmates ate meals and played cards or generally passed the time. Each cell on the lower level opened directly into this center area. Cells on the upper tier opened onto a raised catwalk that encircled the upper level and led to a set of stairs on either side of the central court.

Most of the inmates in the Bravo module were newly sentenced individuals, prone to impulsive acts of violence or suicidal gestures in the opening days of their life behind bars. After months or even years of a drawn out trial proceedings, the finality of a slamming cell door was overwhelming for some inmates.

Vague legal terminology took on its hardened concrete meaning in this part of the prison. You are under arrest. How do you plead? Do you have counsel? Your bail is set. This man is guilty; you must convict. Have you reached a verdict? You are sentenced. The culmination of drawn-out legal proceedings and a sudden loss of identity left many inmates, especially first time offenders, in a vulnerable state of hopelessness, further compounded by the ritualistic confiscation of all personal effects during the remand process. In exchange, the prison issued a matching set of faded prison clothes to each inmate, and he was then escorted to his cell, alone, to begin the sometimes violent process of establishing a new prison identity. Under the weight of this loss of identity, some individuals saw suicide as the only way out.

Avalyn secured the strap of the emergency bag over her shoulder and ran in the direction of the shouting. A crowd of inmates stood over a limp body just outside an open cell on the lower tier. They anxiously separated, allowing Avalyn to see the pale individual. He was young and unkempt with dirty hair, sprawled supine on the floor like a discarded doll.

"He's hung himself," yelled one of the inmates. "He's gone and done it."

Avalyn dropped her bag to the floor and squatted onto one knee. As she reached for the carotid artery, she noted the abrasion across the inmate's anterior neck. She pressed her fingers firmly under the angle of the young man's jaw, feeling for pulsations; then she acted out a series of life-saving maneuvers, largely performed without conscious thought, singularly focused on restoring the flow of blood to the young man's brain. "He has a weak pulse. But no respirations. Hand me the ambu-bag and prepare the A.E.D."

The other nurse handed Avalyn a breathing apparatus made of a mask connected to a squeezable elongated ball used to push air into the lungs of a patient in respiratory arrest. Avalyn placed the mask over the young man's mouth and nose and gave several short breaths. As she gave these breaths, the shadow of a crowd of inmates extended over the scene. Some of the inmates began wailing. Avalyn looked up at an officer and shouted, "Call 911 and secure this mod. These inmates need to be in their cells!"

After several rescue breaths, the victim began to cough. Avalyn stopped assisting with the respirations. The young man, still far from conscious, began taking difficult, irregular breaths ominously accentuated by the resonance of stridor. His blood pressure rose, and his pulse returned, slow but strong. After a minute or two, when Avalyn called his name, he opened his eyes but otherwise remained distant. He persisted in a drowsy, postictal daze for several minutes.

Avalyn and her colleague gave the young man supplemental oxygen, started an IV, and checked his vital signs.

One of the officers exited the young man's cell holding a braided loop meticulously fashioned from strips of cloth torn from bed sheets. "Here's your noose. The other inmates found him with it tied around the railing of the upper bunk."

By the time paramedics arrived, the young man was answering basic questions. Avalyn felt herself relax at the sound of the paramedics being buzzed through the entry port. *This one is lucky*, she thought and she turned to place her rescue supplies back in the emergency bag.

The paramedics from a division of the local fire department arrived in thick department gear and addressed the scene with thorough efficiency. They assisted the young man onto a gurney, which had been lowered to just above floor height. Several straps were pulled across the young man's legs and body to keep him belted on the wheeled gurney.

As he was being secured to the gurney, the young man raised the palm of his hand to his head. "My head hurts," he said with sluggish, slurred words.

"How long has he been talking like this?" asked one of the paramedics.

Before anyone could answer, the young man's eyes rolled backward, and his head fell to the side. His arms and legs began to shake wildly.

One of the paramedics pulled out a mobile phone and extended a cord connected to both the phone and an earpiece. He then called the local emergency room while the other paramedic finished belting the inmate to the gurney. The second paramedic placed an oxygen mask over the young man's face and pushed the gurney toward the door, the wheels vibrating under the rapidly moving stretcher.

The lead paramedic followed behind, speaking rapidly into the mobile phone, "We are en route with a 26-year-old Caucasian male found unresponsive with a cervical ligature approximately twenty minutes ago. He briefly regained consciousness after resuscitative measures and maintained a bradycardic pulse with spontaneous irregular respirations; he has again become unresponsive and is demonstrating generalized tonic-clonic seizure activity; we suspect anoxic brain injury…."

The words used by the paramedic were foreign; very few people in the cell block knew medical terminology, but the meaning was clear. The large concrete-walled cell block fell into respectful stillness as inmates stood in silence behind closed cell doors peering through bars to watch medical personnel exit the arena with a fallen comrade.

Avalyn and her fellow nurse followed the paramedics and officers out of the Bravo module and watched them rapidly wheel the patient down the long corridor. Avalyn knew the young man would likely never again regain consciousness.

The concrete walls of the outer hallway seemed to amplify even hushed conversation between the two as they turned back toward the medical wing of the prison.

The nurse rolled her eyes and said to Avalyn, "Well, it looks like we saved another donor."

Avalyn took a deep breath and nodded to

acknowledge the fact that though many attempted suicides result in brain death, viable organs may be preserved if first responders achieved a rapid restoration of blood flow. She responded, "I don't understand what kind of darkness makes suffocation seem like a welcome alternative, but whatever his reasons, his decision may save another person's life."

"Yeah, let's keep telling ourselves that," the other nurse replied as they were about to part, "but I won't give him credit for adding anything positive to my day."

Suddenly an officer called out from the open door of the segregation control room a few hundred feet down the corridor, "You ladies want to see something cool? We caught Ferguson fishing again."

The nurses mentally pushed the vivid images of the young man's suicide from their minds. Though pressed for time, they walked quickly down the corridor to the segregation module control room. Avalyn had seen fishing before, but the other nurse was newer to the prison and had only heard about the practice.

Avalyn entered the control room first and paused just inside the door to allow her eyes to adjust from the bright, well-lit hallway to the darkness of the control room. The room was illuminated only faintly by a panel of monitors. Each screen was focused on a different cell in the maximum segregation unit, allowing prison security staff to watch and record the activity of every inmate housed in segregation.

The officer sat down at his post and pointed to one of the monitors, "This video was obtained about an hour ago. Keep your eye on Ferguson. He bends down and throws something out the space under his door. Now look at the footage from outside the cells. You will barely see it. Watch for something moving quickly like a mouse darting across the floor. There, see it? Now watch from inside this other cell. That's Mathis; he's in the cell directly across from Ferguson about a hundred feet away. Mathis gets up from his stool when he sees something shoot under his door. Amazing, right? Ferguson threw a small homemade disc a hundred feet right into the cell of Mathis. It's like some life-size game of air hockey. But watch this; it gets even better. Mathis placed something on the disc and here in the open space between the two cells you see a small package inching slowly back toward Ferguson's cell."

"Where did he get fishing line? Is that how it's moving?" asked the nurse.

"Great question. You cannot see it, but the disc was connected to a thin string, almost thread-like, which was dyed to blend in with the floor. Ferguson is pulling the object back to his cell. He's probably going slowly to avoid notice, but he doesn't get away with it. See, the segregation sergeant comes in from the side and confiscates the object."

"Amazing," said the nurse, "do they do this often?"

"All the time. Ferguson is one of the best I've ever seen. He once got a disc over the upper tier rail and bounced the disc off the control wall and back into a cell underneath him on the floor level. I've seen inmates fish for messages, drugs, and sometimes even cell phones.

Funny, huh? Prisoners using *cell* phones?" the officer paused briefly to laugh alone at his own worn out pun. "We find about one of those a week in here."

Avalyn leaned forward as if to study the monitor more closely, "So what was Ferguson fishing for this morning?"

The officer reached for a small package off the desk in front of him, "Just this," he said. He tossed the object up to Avalyn.

Avalyn caught the small bundle. It was a soft object wrapped in newspaper. Avalyn looked puzzled.

The officer said, "Go ahead and open it. Sometimes they wrap it in newsprint to camouflage the package against the grey concrete floor."

Avalyn unwrapped the package and held up the contents in the dim light of the control room. "Instant coffee? It's just small bags of instant coffee."

"I know. It's disappointing. No big score today. Maybe it was just a commissary trade; you know like coffee for ramen noodles or something."

"Well thanks for the show anyway," said Avalyn. But before she turned to leave she looked down at the newspaper clip used as wrapping for the coffee packets. She unfolded the paper and held the outstretched clip under a light on the officer's desk. "What's this?"

The newspaper clipping was an article from the local paper. The headline read, "A Federal Court Grants a Convicted Murderer the Right to Die at His Own Hands." It was the same article Avalyn read over breakfast that very morning. Why this article? Was Mathis passing a message to Ferguson?

Then Avalyn saw something strange on the clipping. Individual letters in the article were faintly circled in pencil. "Look at this. Do you have a pad or scratch paper. I need something to write on?"

The officer pulled a scrap of paper from his desk drawer. Avalyn reached for a pen and scribbled the circled letters on the scrap of paper. Her stomach cramped suddenly in a nervous spasm as the message became clear. She stood up abruptly and stepped back from the officer's desk pointing toward the scribbled note. "What does that mean?"

The officer looked down at the scratch paper and sounded out the message, "s-w-e-e-p-t-o-d-a-y-2-0-0-p-m."

"What happens today at two?" asked Avalyn.

"I don't know. Shift change for a few of the officers working an eight-hour shift occurs at that time. But the inmates are on lockdown or at least restricted to their modules during the change of staff. Maybe it has something to do with this guy Sherman mentioned in the article."

"Sherman is in the infirmary. Why would Mathis or Ferguson be involved with him?"

"Mathis is very influential within the prison. It could be an order. He has run some fairly elaborate schemes from here in segregation. Remember the judge who was busted for taking bribes? That judge was receiving regular payments out of Mathis' bank account, some in the six figure range, all of it coordinated by Mathis from right here in segregation. That's one of the times we caught him using contraband cell phones. The guy had ten different cell phones stashed around his cell, in his mattress, in the hem of his blanket, even had one affixed to the bottom of the toilet bowl."

"So was Sherman involved with these guys?" asked Avalyn.

The officer thought for a moment, "Well, there's no way to know, really. They've all been here a long time. Sherman used to live in Echo mod. I guess he may have had jobs over the years that put him in contact with Mathis or any of the other inmates."

Avalyn asked, "So what was Sherman like back on the mod?"

"Can't really say he stood out. Just one of the regulars, I guess. Although I do remember he spent a lot of time in the gym."

"Was that weird?"

"I don't know. I guess it was strange that he didn't really play ball with the others. He would spend hours by himself, just shooting a basketball, you know, standing at the free throw line shooting baskets. I asked him about it once, 'You getting ready for some big game?' He told me he was just keeping up his skills, something about playing ball with his kid someday."

"So, this message, how would it get outside this area? Who has contact with Mathis or Ferguson?"

"There are plenty of ways to get a message out. It could be passed by officers or medical personnel. We recently caught a substance abuse counselor communicating with family members on the outside for inmates. Custodial inmates from the worker's mod come to clean the area daily. Sometimes the laundry staff sends and receives messages sewn into clothing. The list goes on and on. It blows my mind to think about how many ways these guys get around our security."

Avalyn's eyes lit up, "Wait. Back up. Does the custodial staff sweep this area?"

"Yes. They sweep and mop the segregation area each morning. What are you thinking?"

"The message says sweep today at two. Could he be telling someone to come by his cell at two o'clock?"

"I don't think so. The custodial staff is out of here by eight in the morning. At two this afternoon, the area will be on complete lock-down."

Avalyn placed a hand on her chest. She could feel her heart pounding with increasing force. She looked over at the officer and her fellow nurse and said, "I get the uneasy feeling something bad is going to happen today at two."

"Maybe not," replied her fellow nurse, "they caught the message before it reached Ferguson."

"I would not find that reassuring," said the officer, "Mathis has a hundred other ways to get his way."

Avalyn remembered she left Sherman's cell before giving him his morning medication. She felt suddenly pressed again for time. She patted the officer on the back and said, "Thank you again for the show. If you'll excuse me, I have to go." She reached down to grab her emergency bag and abruptly left the control room.

Avalyn returned to the infirmary. She tossed the

emergency bag onto the nurses' station desk and glanced at the clock. She only had a few minutes to complete her assessments and finish distributing the morning medications. Doctor Brant was nothing if not prompt.

She walked to the medicine cart, which had not been moved from its position in front of cell number twelve. Pills remained atop the cart sitting in a medicine cup. She felt a visceral constriction in her gut as she lifted the medicine cup and began counting the pills. She noticed her hands trembling in response to an intangible fear. Not fear of the inmate; she dreaded what he was forcing her to become. She looked down into the small medicine cup containing a light dose of pain medication, no more than the typical person might take for a common headache or arthritic knees, as well as a blood pressure pill and a strong antacid. The inmate may have asked for assistance in dying, but the orders for a lethal medication would not come until later. She reminded herself that he was not going to die from the medication she was giving him on morning rounds. The medicines she held were only for mild pain, acid reflux, and blood pressure. She had no reason to fear. But something about the act of handing the inmate a cup of pills led Avalyn to an unsettling thought. *What would I do if these pills were lethal? Would I be able to hand him medication if I knew it would cause his death?*

Avalyn gathered her composure. She turned to Vatel who was attentively watching her from a distance.

"Ready to see Mr. Sherman?" asked Vatel.

Avalyn nodded, and Vatel opened the door. Together they entered Joseph Sherman's cell, cell number twelve.

Sherman remained still. He sat erect on his bed staring at the pages of a paperback book; he did not look up.

Avalyn broke the silence, "Good morning, Mr. Sherman. I brought your morning medication."

Sherman responded in an ominous deep tone, "What are they saying about me, Nurse Robbins? I hear I am in the news today. What are they saying?"

Avalyn held out the medicine cup, "Mr. Sherman, you've been in here a long time. You know the rules. I cannot pass messages to inmates."

Sherman accepted the medicine cup and poured the pills into his mouth like an Italian slugging an espresso or a drunk throwing back a shot of whiskey. He handed the paper cup back to Avalyn and spoke again as he licked a finger and turned the page in his book, "I see you are trembling, Nurse Robbins. Something distresses you. Perhaps you heard that I'm going to die today. Does this frighten you?"

The question startled Avalyn. She furrowed her eyebrows as if to ponder the question but recognizing it as either inappropriate or manipulative, she elected to deflect his query. "We are not here to talk about me, Mr. Sherman. Do you need anything before the doctor arrives?"

"Just one thing; will you forgive me any wrong I have caused you?"

"There is nothing for me to forgive, Mr. Sherman. Your crimes are not my concern."

"No, but I once learned that to be free, I must make amends with anyone I may have offended or harmed. If any of my actions cause you distress, please forgive me. If it were within my power, I would make it right."

"Thank you for the gesture. But again, there is nothing owed."

"Then the answer is no, I do not have any needs this morning."

"Mr. Sherman, may I ask you a question about your decision?"

"I anticipated you would eventually ask; what is on your mind?"

"Have you considered other options? You do not have to die alone, you know. I'll call hospice. We have an excellent end-of-life care program. You still have time…"

Sherman interrupted her, "My time is up, Nurse Robbins. Doc has reviewed my options with me. Chemotherapy would prolong my life, but at what cost? I'm not interested in hair loss, mouth sores, or debilitating weakness. Radiation therapy would shrink the tumors, yes, but that simply postpones the inevitable. Experimental treatments may be available, but they exclude people like me from that kind of research. And hospice you say? I do not care to sleep while you all watch me die. The doctor says my best option is just to try beating cancer to the final punch. Consider it a spiritual retribution; my final punishment will be to die alone."

Sherman folded his book in his lap and looked right at Avalyn, "But now that I think about, I do have one wish; will you make me a single promise? When I die will you close my mouth and my eyes? People always seem to die with their mouth and eyes open. It's undignified. Makes people think you died screaming. Promise me you will close my mouth and my eyes before the rigor mortis permanently fixes my state?"

Vatel interjected with a sigh, "A beautiful funeral is no guarantee of heaven."

Sherman looked up, giving Vatel a cold, hate-filled stare, "And wearing a badge is no guarantee of safety."

Avalyn verbally separated the two, "Mr. Sherman, you will be treated with compassion and dignity, just like everyone else."

The conversation was interrupted by a gruff baritone voice echoing out from across the infirmary, "Nuuursse…where is the nurse? Am I paid to sit on my glutes and do nothing? The blight of society is waiting to be seen. Where is my nurse? Come, people. A sloth could move faster than the help in this place."

Vatel articulated the obvious, "Nurse Robbins, I believe Doctor Brant has arrived."

CHAPTER FIVE

THE PHYSICIAN EXPLAINS

"We are simply providing a means to help the man end his suffering. This is not killing or suicide. Murder requires the intentional taking of an innocent human life. Suicide is the desperate act of a depressed person in a moment of hopelessness. You must not call this killing or suicide or even assisted suicide. That would mock this man's suffering and label him as weak."

- Calvin Brant, MD
Prison Physician

Doctor Calvin Brant sat at the nurses' station, his hands briskly tapping at a keyboard as he scanned information on the computer's monitor. He bounced an anxious leg beneath him. Without looking away, he yelled insult-laden orders, "Would someone who is not comatose please get me a list of today's patients."

Avalyn responded to the doctor's urgent instructions with a professional ease. If the insults angered her, she did not show it outwardly. She had known Doctor Brant long enough to know his outward behavior was not directed at her. His requests were usually valid; his methods of asking were not. But those who worked with Doctor Brant graciously tolerated his personality flaws, perhaps out of pity.

Most of the staff considered the rough, insulting, brash way Doctor Brant carried himself to be a reflection of his demoralized soul; Avalyn knew his past and tolerated his behavior much like people tolerate the uncivilized bitterness of a person suffering from a painful disease.

Avalyn felt that Doctor Brant's condescending demeanor was simply a result of his own loss of self-worth. The Doctor had good reason to be bitter, although this bitterness was of his own making. Avalyn knew his story, and whether the events were true or merely embellished gossip, those who knew the tragic past of Doctor Brant had reason to feel sorry for him.

Doctor Brant was once a skilled surgeon, some say nationally-acclaimed, who lost his license and his reputation one night by attempting to perform an emergent gallbladder surgery on a young woman while he was impaired, supposedly from drinking at a dinner party. During the procedure, he had lacerated a major blood vessel, and the patient bled to death on the table. Years later, after lawsuits, professional rehabilitation programs, and a period of probation, he was granted a provisional medical license to practice exclusively in the state prison system. The practice paid his bills but did little for his self-esteem. Condescension was a cover for his insecurity; he intimidated nurses, ridiculed inmates, and demeaned the security staff. He became professionally reclusive, sitting alone at meetings. He usually discarded invitations, sparse though they were, to dinner gatherings with other physicians.

Physically he was short with a stocky, almost square build and persistently hunched shoulders as if his whole body had bent forward under the weight of some penance. He wore a pair of round tinted glasses that accentuated his large beak-like nose, and he dressed in a brown wool sport coat that had a unique, musty smell. The only real wardrobe change from one day to the next was his tie. On this day his tie was black.

For reasons about which Avalyn could only speculate, the subject of euthanasia fascinated Doctor Brant. He had become a medical spokesman for the death with dignity movement and lobbied the state and the federal governments to pass laws protecting physicians who assisted terminally ill individuals in ending their own lives. When Joseph Sherman first submitted a request for physician-assisted suicide, it was Doctor Brant who had signed the prescription. He had been interviewed on news shows and had published opinion essays in popular magazines. Despite a horrid bedside manner, in the media Calvin Brant, MD, came across as a compassionate champion for the terminally ill; he was articulate, firm against opponents, and if nothing else, passionate about his belief that some lives are no longer worthy of continuing.

Avalyn approached the doctor apologetically, "Forgive me, sir. I do not yet have all the vitals recorded."

Doctor Brant was unsympathetic, "Am I right in saying that this computer is used more for chatting and shopping than for doing actual work? How hard is it to take a blood pressure and type the result into the record?"

"We were interrupted by a suicide attempt. An inmate coded and required CPR; he likely will not make it."

"How much time does it take to run a code, Nurse Robbins? I'll tell you how long. Ten minutes, tops. If your patient has no pulse at ten minutes, stop. Don't waste your time on a person who makes it clear he wants to check out on his own time."

Doctor Brant did not pause for a reaction. He pulled a stethoscope from his coat pocket, wrapped it around his neck, and walked up to cell one, "Guard, open the door please."

Vatel slid a key into the slot and stated kindly, "With pleasure, sir."

As Vatel leaned forward to open the door, Doctor Brant, visibly annoyed by the delay, saw the officer's name sewn above his left pocket, "Vatel, huh? Sounds foreign. You get one of those online degrees? I guess you only need a grade-school education to work here these days."

Vatel responded with a grin, "You undervalue yourself, sir."

Brant failed to appreciate the slur, which he walked right into, but Avalyn caught Vatel's quick wit. She made sure Brant was not looking when she gave Vatel an approving nod.

Together the three of them entered each cell. Doctor Brant personally greeted each patient, but every comment following his greeting was blatantly impersonal, "This leg is worse…the liver is failing…the arm needs to see orthopedics."

The encephalopathic in room four, as Doctor Brant called him, was quietly sleeping under the sedative effect of the injection given earlier. "Leave him to his dreams," said the doctor.

Doctor Brant moved efficiently. He was in and out of each cell in a matter of minutes, sometimes seconds. He paused between rooms only long enough to give instructions regarding changes to a medication or to issue instructions on what he expected to be done for the inmate.

But Brant paused in front of cell twelve. He did not

reveal his thoughts. He just paused as if silently rehearsing lines before going on stage. Through the window of the cell he could see Joseph Sherman sitting upright in his bed reading a book with his back to the door. "The lock please," said Doctor Brant.

When Sherman heard the key working his lock he closed his book and swung his legs off the edge of the bed, "Good morning, Doc."

Unlike his dry greeting with other inmates Doctor Brant seemed to greet Joseph Sherman warmly, "Today is the day, my friend. The courts have granted your request. Your life is now solely in your own hands. How do you wish to proceed?"

Sherman took a long, thoughtful breath as he raised his eyes to meet the doctor's eyes, "Do you think I should, Doctor?"

"The decision is yours. You have an aggressive disease. As I have told you before, terminal cancer is a hard way to go. If it were me, I would be glad just to know I had an option."

"How long do I have, Doc, if…you know…if I don't go through with it?"

Doctor Brant squinted, taking on an expression of concern; he stroked his chin and answered, "Your oncologist estimated less than six months of meaningful life; that was two months ago. You are already having trouble swallowing solid food. At some point you will not be able to swallow the medicine at all and at that point your opportunity for a dignified death will have passed."

"How long does it take for the medicine to work?"

"Ten to thirty minutes."

"Does it cause pain?" asked Sherman.

"Absolutely not," answered the doctor, "The medication is a high-dose sedative. It is similar to what we use before surgery to relax the patients. You will not feel a thing. It's all quite peaceful."

"Can it fail? I mean…is there a chance the drugs only work long enough to kill my brain and leave me here like a vegetable?"

"The regimen is safe, I can assure you. The medication you will receive is the same medicine used by thousands of patients who wished to voluntarily terminate their lives. There has never been even one recorded failure once the medication was ingested."

"But what if I throw up?"

"Good question," said the doctor. "You will receive a nausea medication to take before the sleeping pills. This will prevent you from vomiting."

"So is it pills or a drink or what?"

Doctor Brant began swaying in a non-verbal declaration of impatience, "This visit is getting long, Mr. Sherman. I can come back tomorrow if you still have questions."

"No," Sherman interjected, "I'm ready. But would you have the power to give me one more thing doctor? May I have caregivers to provide company when the time comes?"

Doctor Brant turned to Vatel, "I'll defer to security for an answer to that question."

Vatel slapped the back of one hand into the palm of

his opposite hand, "Forgive me for being blunt, Mr. Sherman, but this is a prison. A lethal drug behind these walls is no different than a loaded gun."

Sherman interrupted, "I can assure you all, I would never use my medication to hurt another person."

Vatel shot back, "Excuse me, Mr. Sherman; it is my understanding that you are in prison for reasons that would suggest otherwise."

Sherman's face became tight and red. He raised a finger toward Vatel, "I am a dying man. What right do you have to stand there like some righteous judgmental pig telling me why I'm in prison?"

Doctor Brant broke in, "Mr. Sherman, maintain your composure. I can speak with the superintendent about your request."

"No more delays," said Mr. Sherman, "Just give me the drug. I have no more use for this place."

Doctor Brant once again squinted behind his large round glasses, "You are a brave man, Mr. Sherman. The stories they write about you will show that even a prison cannot contain a man's freedom to choose the manner and time of his passing."

Doctor Brant exited the cell with his head bowed. He returned to the nurses' desk taking slow thoughtful steps like an undertaker. Avalyn and Vatel quietly followed.

Doctor Brant sat back down at the nurses' desk and began typing what appeared to be a list of orders.

Avalyn watched the screen. She silently read each line as it appeared. As the meaning of the list became clear, her head and legs felt suddenly weak; she pulled out a rolling stool and sat down beside the doctor.

Doctor Brant spoke to her in a hushed voice, "This afternoon the pharmacist will deliver a drug called secobarbital for Mr. Sherman. There should be exactly ninety pills. It comes in capsule form but the dose in each capsule is much too small for the intended effect. Since swallowing ninety capsules is impractical, not to mention problematic for controlling absorption, we use the following work-around: all of the capsules must be opened and poured into a cup; the powder is bitter and should be mixed into a sugary drink; then the entire amount must be ingested in a brief amount of time, otherwise he may fall asleep before taking the entire dose. Do you understand?"

Avalyn nodded understanding but responded slowly, "Are you saying I must prepare the medication?"

"Absolutely not," Doctor Brant replied, "for better or worse the law only allows the patient to prepare the mixture. No one else may participate."

"But who will actually hand him the pills?"

"You will. At the afternoon medication pass you should administer the pills to Mr. Sherman along with a cup of juice and twenty five milligrams of promethazine to prevent nausea. Please ensure he understands these instructions."

"Doesn't it bother you that Mr. Sherman still has so many questions? Do you really think he's ready for this?"

Doctor Brant shrugged, "They always have questions. This may be the single most important decision a person makes. His questions are not unusual or unexpected. To me it is a sign that he is ready. Sherman has thought this through. He is ready."

Avalyn heard the words but did not acknowledge agreement. She stared at Doctor Brant as if trying to comprehend the full meaning of his instructions. The thought of handing a lethal dose of medication to another person was incomprehensible. Her mind fluctuated between partial thoughts, not complete opinions or conclusions, just an uncoordinated mix of beliefs and experiences, like trying to determine how something tastes without waiting for the finish. She was being asked to do something that did not entirely seem right, but she could not articulate specifically why. She looked up and said, "I don't know if I can be a part of this, sir."

"Then you need to call someone who can," Doctor Brant replied.

Avalyn stumbled over her words, "That's unnecessary. I could do it…I just don't think…I mean…I don't know if this is right…just to let a man kill himself while we stand by and watch. It's like I'm being asked to hand him the gun."

"This is not suicide, Nurse Robbins. Our patient is not depressed; he is dying. His life-span is no longer open-ended. He is competent and has asked for help. His request is legal. You have the right to excuse yourself from his care, but you cannot obstruct his request for a dignified death."

Avalyn said, "I understand his medical condition. I have taken care of many patients who need palliative care, and here in the infirmary, we provide every dying inmate with the highest care possible. I have held the hand of many of them even as they passed; I have just never actually caused their death."

Doctor Brant tapped his foot as if readying himself to leap from the chair. He pointed a finger at Avalyn, "Hear me clearly. You are not causing Mr. Sherman's death. None of us is causing his death. He is dying of cancer. When I sign his death certificate, it will read that he died of a terminal metastatic sarcoma. Not murder. Not suicide. He is terminally ill. The outcome is certain. You cannot cause his death any more than you caused his cancer."

Avalyn became apologetic, "I'm sorry, Doctor. I know you've thought this through, but for me it's all new. It just seems like a short-cut version of health care."

Doctor Brant looked at the ceiling as if searching for a simple way to make his point, "May I tell you a story about my favorite dog? It's a true story. Maximus was my best friend. In the darkest hour of my life when others abandoned me, Max never gave up. He remained at my side when I was at my lowest. With the nudge of his cold nose and sloppy morning lick across my face, he reminded me I had something for which to live. I owe that dog my life. When he was well along in years, he developed a kidney problem which left him weak and in visible discomfort. Having been at my side no matter what for all those years I could not bear to watch him suffer in his final days. So I met with the veterinarian. He helped us determined a time and place to grant old Max the ultimate dignity of a peaceful death, a good death.

Max passed peacefully. My question for you is this: why should we not be able to offer this same level of care to our patients? Should we treat our pets better than we do our own patients?"

Avalyn tried to understand the doctor's analogy, but her own experience did not resonate with his, "My dad took our old family dog out behind the barn and shot him. I still remember the gun blast. I closed myself in my room and cried every day for a week. My dad told me to get over it; he said it was the humane thing to do."

"I am not suggesting we shoot our patients," argued Doctor Brant.

"But are you suggesting we should treat people like we treat animals?"

The doctor laughed, "On the contrary, I'm suggesting that we are inhumane to the extent we treat our sick worse than we treat our animals."

"But animals can't tell us what they want."

"Animals can let us know when they suffer, and we do not turn a deaf ear," said Doctor Brant, "How much more should we be sensitive to the suffering of fellow human beings?"

Avalyn shrugged her shoulders and looked toward cell number twelve. She could see Joseph Sherman sitting up in his bed facing away from the window.

Doctor Brant noticed her diverted attention, "You disagree with me?"

"It just feels like a step toward something sinister," Avalyn said, "I understand that even Nazi doctors were told they were doing something good."

"Ah, the infamous slippery slope. You think if we help one person end his suffering there will be no stopping evil forces that seek to euthanize every mentally ill, elderly, or unwanted person?"

Avalyn shook her head, "I can't really say what I think, but I can tell you what bothers me: I don't want to look back on this day and wonder if I killed a man or helped him commit suicide."

Doctor Brant raised an eyebrow. His lips tightened as if preparing to say something most serious, "We are simply providing a means to help the man end his suffering. This is not killing or suicide. Murder requires the intentional taking of an innocent human life. Suicide is the desperate act of a depressed person in a moment of hopelessness. You must not call this killing or suicide or even assisted suicide. That would mock this man's suffering and label him as weak."

Vatel stood near the desk patiently listening to the conversation. Intermittently he furrowed his eyebrows revealing an inward discomfort with the ideas being discussed. Finally he interjected himself, "Excuse me sir, I am not a health care professional, but is there not something in your Hippocratic Oath that prevents you from taking such action?"

Doctor Brant leaned back in his chair and folded his arms looking at Vatel with a contemptuous grin, "An oath taken before Greek gods by physicians who lived over two thousand years ago seems a little out of date don't you think?"

Vatel shook his head, "I believe the age of a document

gives it more credibility, not less; wisdom is passed down through generations; foolishness dies with a fool."

The doctor's face reddened slightly. He had clearly had this conversation with others and felt no reluctance to a battle of wits with a non-medical corrections officer, "So you believe I should hold to the oath? Would you agree then that I should hold to the entire oath? That as a doctor I should bow before Aesclapius and Apollo and bar women from becoming doctors and forbid contraception and let the man with a kidney stone suffer his lot? And, while we're at it, should I promise never to use my skill and knowledge to end the suffering of a terminally ill man? Is that what you are saying?"

Vatel was unmoved, the barrage of words intended to humiliate him bounced off like water hitting a stone wall, "Doctors who take that oath, I presume, would prefer to be trusted rather than feared."

Doctor Brant removed the glasses from his face and pointed them at Vatel as if making a physical gesture to underscore an intellectual point, "We are not killing this man. He is being allowed to voluntarily terminate his own life on his terms. Why can't you get that through your thick skull?

Officer Vatel took a calm step toward the doctor; he lowered his voice and asked, "Tell us doctor, if *he* is ending his life, why are *you* here?"

Doctor Brant rose to his feet. He placed his glasses back on his face and planted both fists firmly on the desk, "People who try to end their own lives make a terrible mess. Have you ever had to clean up after a self-inflicted gunshot wound? That's why you need doctors. With a well-chosen medication, a doctor can grant a person a perfectly peaceful passing. Our knowledge of how to prolong a life comes also with the knowledge of how to end a life." He pointed a finger at Vatel and added, "That is why only doctors are qualified to wield the syringe."

Officer Vatel held out both hands as if welcoming a guest, "Sir, since you are needed, I insist you must not leave. Please, stay with your team until the work is done."

Doctor Brant snatched his coat which had been lying across the edge of his chair. He walked around the desk to a sink and began washing his hands, "You do your job, and I'll do mine. I do not have the interest or time to hold hands with dying antisocial psychopaths."

"You are mistaken sir," replied Vatel, "your hands are the ones that have the power to heal; my job is only public safety."

The doctor pulled a paper towel. He glared briefly at Vatel as he dried his hands. Then he tossed the wadded paper in the waste can, "If you want to be in law enforcement, go to the police academy. You're a guard. They do not even issue you a weapon. Seems like a security gig at the mall would be more appropriate for you."

Vatel stood proudly erect, "With respect, sir, I'm an officer not a guard."

The doctor raised his hands to the ceiling, "Ah, of course, an officer; I should have known; guards watch over things of value." With that Doctor Brant turned and walked out of the infirmary.

Vatel watched the doctor depart and said under his breath, "There goes a man who washes his hands in water but dries them in the dirt."

Avalyn handed Vatel a paper cup of cold water, "Don't let him get to you, Officer."

Vatel took a sip, "Thank you, Mrs. Robbins. But I was more worried that he was getting to you."

"Not anymore; it's like my grandpa used to say, 'You can't out-puke a buzzard.'"

"So what are you going to do, Mrs. Robbins? Are you going to give Joseph Sherman the pills?"

"I don't know," Avalyn thought for a moment, "Would you think less of me if I did?"

Vatel allowed a slow broad smile to grow across his face, "I think if it is God who sends you on an errand, He will pay your expenses."

Avalyn nodded, "Thank you, Vatel, but may I ask you a personal question?"

Vatel pulled up a chair and sat down, "Mrs. Robbins, generally speaking you may ask me anything. What is your question?"

CHAPTER SIX

CHOOSING SIDES

"...in those days you had to worry that someone had paid more for your death than you paid for your life."

- Frantz Vatel
Correctional Officer

Before Avalyn could ask her question, a roving officer entered through a back door to the infirmary. He wore a blue uniform with the name JONES stitched above his left pocket. He was whistling and flipping a pair of handcuffs over his extended finger. He saw Avalyn and Officer Vatel sitting by the nurses' desk and said in a thick southern accent, "Good mornin', you slackers. You got inmate Sherman here? Is he still breathin'?"

"Very funny. Are you still getting your jokes off cereal boxes?" answered Avalyn. She pointed toward Sherman's cell, "He's in twelve. What's up?"

"He's got a professional visit. A lawyer type is here. Says he's Sherman's attorney. Probably here to give the legal last rights or draft a final will and testament. Word has it he's dyin' today. You guys part of that? Wait, don't answer that. I don't even want to know. Must be a weird day to be on shift 'round here."

Officer Vatel walked over to cell twelve and used his heavy key to open the cell door. Sherman was still sitting on the side of his bed. The sudden opening of the door startled him, "What's the problem, Officer?"

Vatel laughed at Sherman's response, "There is no problem, Mr. Sherman. You have a pro-visit. Please step out of the room and face the wall."

Sherman rose slowly and stepped casually out of the

cell. He turned toward the outside of his window and leaned forward with outstretched hands against the wall.

Officer Jones patted down Sherman's arms, legs, and torso to ensure he was free of weapons or contraband. Then he cuffed Sherman's hands in front of him and asked, "Mr. Sherman you got any medical problems that would prevent us from walkin' to the consultation room?"

Sherman grinned at Officer Jones and said sarcastically, mimicking his southern accent, "Why, I'm the picture of health today, Officer; a walk wit' the likes of you would be just fine."

Then Sherman turned to Vatel, this time speaking in his normal voice, "Officer, would you ask the custodial inmate to mop my room while I'm out? I spilled some of my breakfast. These shoes are sticking to the floor."

Vatel shook his head, "That request must be submitted directly to the custodial staff. Put a request in the box when you return. They pick up the requests each morning."

"Well, that might work, but do I need to remind you that I may not be here in the morning?" Then he smiled and said in jest, "Better be nice to me; I'm about to speak to my lawyer."

Vatel stood up straight. Lawyers did not scare him, and he recognized Sherman was only joking; but for a moment he paused as if weighing in the balance the two virtues of justice: a professional impartiality that enforced rules; and a humanitarian compassion that recognized when rules no longer apply. Avalyn could not tell what gave him pause, but she heard him answer with an uncharacteristic whisper, "I will see what I can do."

Officer Jones led Sherman to the back door of the infirmary. He pushed a button next to the door and spoke into the intercom, "Jones here at the infirmary door number two with Inmate Sherman to the consultation room."

The magnetic lock clicked. Jones pushed the door open and hollered to Vatel, "Should be back in an hour."

Vatel keyed his radio, "Control. This is Med Seg. Be advised Inmate Sherman has left the infirmary for a pro-visit, and Doctor Brant has exited the infirmary."

A sergeant responded over the radio, "Control. Affirmative. Sherman to consultation room. And I understand the doctor is clear of Medical Segregation. Did he mind his manners this morning?"

Vatel smiled at Avalyn and again keyed his mike, "Negative, control. In fact Med Seg recommends a count at control's discretion before further staff clearance."

"Understood. Count advised."

Avalyn tilted her head to the side cutting her eyes toward Vatel as if to communicate that she knew Vatel was up to something altogether crafty. He was speaking to the control sergeant in a form of code, and she knew exactly what it meant.

"What are you up to, Officer?" asked Avalyn.

Vatel laughed deeply, "Just buying the good doctor a little time to get his affairs in order before passing into the free world." He pulled a chair up to the desk and said, "Now, what did you want to ask me?"

Avalyn looked directly at Vatel for a moment. She did not immediately speak. She just looked at him as if to confirm that he was fully attentive. Then she spoke in a slow, almost reserved manner, "You know these inmates, and you know Mr. Sherman. You know the suffering he has caused. As far as I can tell, he deserves to be here. Maybe he deserves worse; God only knows the full extent of his crimes. But I don't think he should suffer more than the average person just because he is in prison. I feel like he may have the right to end his own life. But I don't know if I can hand him the drugs to do it. It just feels like I'm being asked to play the role of an executioner. I can't do that; I won't do that. But I am trained to administer prescribed medication and provide healthcare. That's what nurses do. And here a life-ending drug has been prescribed for a patient on my shift. I just don't know what to do."

Vatel's eyes squinted in warm understanding, "There are no short cuts are there, Mrs. Robbins? The path that first seems easy can become full of thorns."

Avalyn looked puzzled, "Do you mean that it is easier to give the drugs or that it is easier not to give the drugs?"

"Did I ever tell you about my parents?" asked Vatel.

Avalyn shrugged her shoulders, "I thought you were adopted."

"Yes, this is true. My birth parents died in Haiti when I was a baby. I have been told they were influential people, my parents, I mean. My dad was a land owner and my mother was a teacher in a mountain village. At some point they both became very ill and went to the local

Bokor for help; I think you would call the man a witchdoctor. The Bokor asked for a large amount of money to cure them, which they paid. But in those days you had to worry that someone had paid more for your death than you paid for your life. I am told that a soldier, a general in the military, had fallen in love with my mother and paid the witchdoctor to have my father poisoned. The Bokor mixed poison into the medication he gave to my father, but unfortunately, because mom was also ill, she took the poisoned medication as well. They both died that night."

"I'm sorry to hear this, Vatel. I never knew," said Avalyn.

"Don't be sorry, Mrs. Robbins; be warned. The witchdoctor is feared, not trusted, because he does not pick a side; he manipulates both life and death for his own benefit. Many people pay the witchdoctor to do what others will not do, but the money is handed to him with trembling hands. You are different. You are trusted because you only work on the side of life. These men may not always like you, but they respect you because they know you cannot be bought. If I may say, what you decide to do today will not affect what happens to Mr. Sherman; his end is already determined; but what you decide to do will affect you, and it will affect the trust these men have in you."

As Avalyn listened to Vatel, she felt anxiety rising up her spine. Her shoulders tightened. She had every reason to believe that Vatel was right; inmates in the infirmary knew what was happening in cell twelve. Avalyn looked around her. She felt her mouth going dry, inhibiting her ability to speak or swallow. The inmates could each be seen from her chair; and each of them seemed to be looking at her, watching, if not directly, at least in short glances. Avalyn knew that everything Vatel said was true. Sherman's decision was no longer a private matter; every one of her patients knew what she had been asked to do.

Vatel noticed Avalyn's suddenly flushed appearance, "Are you ok, Mrs. Robbins?"

"Yes, I'm fine," she answered, "I just need a little time to think. They do not teach courses on this kind of thing in nursing school."

Vatel leaned back and opened his eyes widely, "I am surprised. What *do* they teach?"

Avalyn laughed nervously, "Oh, we took a few ethics classes. People talked, sometimes argued, about the many sides of an issue. Mostly we just reviewed cases and talked about big ethical problems; you know, things like why it is wrong to experiment on people like they did in Tuskegee, and how prisoners are a vulnerable population. We had one class called 'When to Pull the Plug' about helping families decide when to end life support. One time we did talk about what we should do if a doctor asked us to give a lethal dose of morphine to a patient who was dying of some dreaded disease. I suppose it was sort of like this case. But no one gave us answers. There were only ambiguous guidelines. Nothing on the test about assisting a suicide. And the classes all ended the same way."

Vatel raised his eyebrows, "How did the classes end?"

"They all ended with the teacher saying something vague and neutral like, 'There are no right or wrong answers, in the end you must stay true to yourself and do what's right for you.'"

Vatel nodded, "Ok. And what is right for you, Mrs. Robbins?"

Avalyn gave a half-faced glinting smile, "You are starting to sound like my teacher. What's right for me is a break. Look at the time. You know I love a good discussion, but there is a cup of coffee in the nurses' lounge waiting for me."

Vatel glanced down at his monitor, "Before you run off, come take a look. The good doctor is trying to leave."

Avalyn slid her chair over to the officer's closed circuit monitor. On the black-and-white screen she could see Doctor Brant entering into the sally port on his way out of the prison. He placed his badge into the tray slot and stood momentarily before the large mirrored glass.

A control officer spoke over the facility intercom, "Inmate count now in progress. Please hold all movement. All posts report your census."

On the monitor Doctor Brant could be seen knocking on the mirrored glass and raising his hands in a gesture of displeasure.

Avalyn looked at Vatel. She raised both eyebrows and bit her lip, "Well, what have you done to stir the hornet's nest this time?"

CHAPTER SEVEN

STAGES OF GRIEF

"You have control...I know you will let me pass when the time is right...but I am anxious to leave, and with your permission and help, I could be going."

- Calvin Brant, MD
Prison Physician

Doctor Brant heard the order for an inmate count over the intercom. He looked up at the speaker in the ceiling of the sally port; he cocked his head like a puppy hearing a strange voice for the first time.

The room in which he was standing was soundproof except for the intercom. Doctor Brant was caught between two locked doors. The door behind him was locked. The exit door before him was locked. Doctor Brant stood in the middle. Control over his ability to depart was entirely in the hands of someone he could not see, a person on the other side of a one-way mirror.

Doctor Brant peered at the mirrored window. He squinted and cupped his hands over his eyes to block the light in an attempt to see the individual behind the glass, the one who held him in limbo. But he could not see beyond the pane. The harder he looked, the more he saw only an angry reflection of himself.

This moment of forced self-reflection annoyed Doctor Brant. He pounded on the glass and raised his hands in a gesture of displeasure, "Why this delay? I need to move on. Who is in control here?"

A control officer's voice responded over the intercom, "Doctor, we are on lock-down until all inmates are counted. Stand by."

The doctor yelled toward the speaker as if responding

to a voice from above, "I can't believe this is happening. Do I look like an inmate to you? Give me my keys and let me through."

"With respect sir, inmates sometimes dress like staff in order to escape. You will be released once all inmates are accounted for."

Doctor Brant grimaced while shaking his head. He leaned back against the cinderblock wall opposite the mirrored glass and shouted, "Respect? You call this respect? I am Doctor Brant, not some half-brained convict dressed like me. You are holding me out of spite. That's all this is, pure spite. You know exactly who I am. And you are sitting there in your high-throne control room acting like a god who has no real worshipers. You think that wielding your authority will somehow earn my respect. If that is true, then forget it. Hold me here all day if you wish. Enjoy this opportunity and take some pleasure in watching a professional who actually graduated from college wait on you."

A collection of officers gathered in the control room behind the mirrored glass, each of them drawn by the promise of an unforgettable show. Many of them had been insulted by Doctor Brant before. This rare opportunity to see him perform a monologue of his best insults while being recorded on camera in a locked room was irresistible. Their motivation was not entirely vindictive. Vengeance may have provided motivation, but payback was not the goal. A morning inmate count was, in fact, a part of the daily routine. And the counts were random to prevent prisoners from detecting a pattern within which an escape could be planned. The fact that this count happened to occur at the very moment the doctor was standing in the sally port was, in the mind of most officers, just a fortuitous coincidence. But no one objected, because this twist of fate provided a rare opportunity for the officers to see the doctor at his unfiltered worst. Thus the officers succumbed to a predictable human trait whereby the suffering of an individual becomes entertainment for a crowd, especially when the one suffering has himself played the role of an oppressor.

Doctor Brant looked at his watch. He began to rock impatiently on his feet from heel to toe. "How long is this going to take? Are the guards counting on their fingers?"

He paused for an answer, but the inner sanctum of the sally port remained silent. Had he been able to hear them he would have heard the officers laughing loudly at his jeers, often applauding at his one-line jabs. One of them shouted encouragement as if cheering on an evangelist, "Preach it, brother. Tell us what you think."

Doctor Brant could not hear or see his audience. He looked up at the intercom speaker, "You cannot hold me here all day. We all have work to do. What megalomaniacal sadomasochistic tyrant is running this preposterous operation? What do you want from me? Is this a toll booth? What's the fee?"

He forcefully reached into his pocket and pulled out a twenty dollar bill and slid it into the slot, "Here's a tip. A little something for your trouble. Now let me pass."

The twenty dollar bill slid silently back through the

slot, a rejected bribe.

Doctor Brant grabbed the money. He pounded his fist on the mirrored glass and cried out, "This delay is a violation of my time. I demand to speak to the superintendent immediately."

An officer's voice responded over the intercom, "I will make the superintendent aware of your request sir."

"I'll tell you what you can do. Make him aware you need a demotion. How do you justify keeping a free person incarcerated in a locked porch for half an hour while you sit there checking your rectal integrity? Let me out of here."

He paused for a breath after several minutes of angry attempts at intimidating or shaming his way out. He took a deep breath and changed his tone, "Listen, you understand this is not about me. I am concerned about my patients. Here I'll show you." He held up a small rectangular paper with the name of an inmate and the name of some medication written in notoriously horrible doctor script, "I have to get this prescription to our pharmacy. If you could just hand me my car keys and let me through I can make sure this patient receives his medication."

There was still no response. The room remained in cold silence except for the sporadic rumbling bang of a distant prison door.

Doctor Brant squinted as he looked into the mirrored glass, as if trying again to see beyond his reflection. It is impossible to know what he was thinking at that point; he did not say anything more. He merely stood for a few moments, silent, looking at his reflection. After a few minutes his shoulders sank as if to acknowledge a release of control. He looked back over his shoulder into the prison; then he looked out the exit toward a waiting room full of individuals who sat out of ear-shot in bored silence, unaware or disinterested in his situation. An officer later said it appeared as though the doctor just gave up. He just stood there contemplating his predicament of being caught somewhere between the misery of prison and the joy of freedom, trapped by the will of someone he knew existed but could not see.

Finally Doctor Brant leaned back against the wall opposite the mirrored window and slid down into a seated position with his legs extended. He folded his hands in his lap and offered up a sort of supplication, "You have a job to do, I understand; my needs are not as important as the institution's priorities. Security comes first. You have control of the door, I know you will let me pass when the time is right for everyone; but I am anxious to leave, and with your permission and help, I could be going."

As soon as Doctor Brant uttered the final words, the exit door buzzed open and a set of car keys appeared in the tray slot. A voice spoke over the intercom, "Good day, sir."

CHAPTER EIGHT

COFFEE BREAK WITH THE NURSES

"I believe every death, just like every life, has an impact on others, probably hundreds of others. Nobody likes taking care of a dying person. It's physically demanding, it's expensive, it's emotionally draining for the caregiver, and demoralizing to the dying person. But caring for them is the honorable thing to do; an honorable death is one that has a positive impact on others and leaves grieving survivors with at least the self-respect of knowing they fought the effects of death to the end."

- Sharon Ballantine, RN
Prison Booking Nurse

Avalyn craved calories and caffeine, but more than that she needed a break, a respite to recover from the stresses of the morning's events. She made her way to the nurses' lounge, a small suite converted from an old records room off the medical wing.

Decades' worth of paper charts had been removed from the windowless storage-area-turned-break-room, but the musty smell of old paper hung in the air like tobacco in an old smokers' lounge. The room now had a small kitchenette with a microwave and refrigerator. Two tattered leather couches lined the walls at a ninety-degree angle; a wooden table had been placed between the couches on which sat a telephone and a few out-of-date magazines. A round, unsteady, pub-height table stood in the center of the room, and a flat screen television occupied the wall opposite the couches.

Two nurses sat at the round table eating rewarmed food from home. They were facing the television, which was muted at the time, watching a national news show. As Avalyn entered the room, one of the nurses pulled a third chair up to the table, "Come join us. They say we are going to be on the news in a few minutes."

Avalyn poured herself a cup of coffee and sat down at the table. Taking her first sip, she inadvertently splashed coffee on her scrub top. The sensation of burning hot fluid hit her suddenly in her upper chest. She instinctively pushed back from the table and leaned forward to separate the saturated cloth from her skin. Having caught her breath, she went to the sink to wash off her shirt with cold water.

Tabitha, one of the two nurses at the table, a slightly overweight woman of short stature with round cheeks that accentuated a broad smile and an amiable personality, pushed herself back from the table as well and grabbed a paper towel. She helped Avalyn clean up the spilled coffee, and when she saw the stain on Avalyn's shirt, she asked, "Do you have spare scrubs?"

Avalyn rubbed the blemish with a moist rag, "No. I'll be wearing this stain the rest of the day."

The other nurse at the table, a woman in her mid-fifties named Sharon, did not move from her seat during the coffee incident; she just watched as she took bites of lukewarm noodles. Her serious countenance and calm demeanor, not to be confused with flippant disregard for Avalyn's spill, merely characterized her overall personality. She had been in the trenches, so to speak, for a long time. Her permanently furrowed somber facial features reflected not so much her age as her experience working the booking areas of the prison. She was the front line medical professional who met hardened, angry, manipulative criminals upon their entry into the prison. Sharon sat in calm contemplation enjoying her meal; then, when she was ready, she spoke what was on her mind without inhibition, since social graces were rarely her concern. She swallowed her last bite and asked, "Is it true? Are they going to let Sherman kill himself?"

"Doctor Brant activated the orders this morning. He left instructions about how the inmate should prepare the drug and take it, supposedly this afternoon."

Tabitha raised her open palms as if pronouncing a blessing. She spoke with syllables extended for emphasis almost like a song, "For all his faults, that Doctor Brant is a man sent from heaven."

Avalyn raised an eyebrow, "Why do you say that?"

"My daddy died last year after a long bout of the Alzheimer's. He declined slowly for years. In the end he did not know me and, to be honest, I didn't know him. On the day of his funeral I had a hard time even resurrecting memories of my daddy the way I wanted to remember him, like he'd want me to remember him. As much as I hate to say it, I wish my daddy had a doctor who cared enough to offer to help him pass peacefully before it got so bad."

"I'm sorry you lost your dad," Avalyn said.

Sharon, however, took a deep, thoughtful breath. She nodded in such a way as to signify understanding, but not necessarily agreement, "You will just have to forgive my mid-western Catholic upbringing. I understand this is a sensitive matter, but it is never acceptable to intentionally kill an innocent human being."

Tabitha interrupted, "But what if the person asks for help and wants to die?"

"Then we help, but not by killing, we relieve suffering and address fears. Let me ask you this: how is a man who wants to end his life because he fears a cancer any different than the man I heard about this morning who tried to kill himself because he fears being in prison? I cannot be judgmental and treat one man differently than another simply because he is depressed over a temporary problem rather than a terminal problem. Their diagnosis is the same; it's fear. Fear of the unknown."

Avalyn asked, "But what if the patient cannot experience fear. Like Tabitha's dad or someone who is in a coma. When a person is no longer aware they even exist, how can we say they are afraid?"

"True, I suppose a patient may lose consciousness; but he or she does not lose his or her dignity as a human being. When a person becomes an invalid, the burden of dignity falls back to the caregiver. It's like when parents care for a baby. It would be a very callous person who says that a baby has no dignity because he or she is dependent on others. It is the inherent dignity of the child that motivates attentive parents to care for the child. This is love. Unconditional care rendered to helpless souls is the essence of human love. If this is how human beings are expected to treat infant persons who have only the potential for a full life, how can we say it is inhumane to care for dependent persons who have lived a full life and, in the final moments, again require the full attention of others?"

Tabitha listened. She grimaced the way people do when something only makes partial sense, "I agree that people have value. If I didn't think that, I wouldn't take care of the offenders in this place, but when a person's bondage to a broken body limits their freedom, isn't freeing them from that bondage the more honorable thing to do?"

Sharon smirked, "More honorable? Don't you mean easier? I believe every death, just like every life, has an impact on others, probably hundreds of others. Nobody likes taking care of a dying person. It's physically demanding, it's expensive, it's emotionally draining for the caregiver, and demoralizing to the dying person. But caring for them is the honorable thing to do; an honorable death is one that has a positive impact on others and leaves grieving survivors with at least the self-respect of knowing they fought the effects of death to the end."

"But think of the cost of that care," Tabitha replied, "I mean for a prisoner who is sentenced for life anyway; it's cheaper to die in prison than to live in prison, especially with a terminal illness. Think about it. The suicide pills cost what? A hundred dollars, maybe? If a man is in jail for the remainder of his life, how many thousands upon thousands of public dollars will be spent on futile medical care? I know many law-abiding, tax-paying families who are wondering how they will pay their own medical bills. Why should they have to pay for him too? A hundred bucks for a man who wants to die with dignity strikes me as a good deal all the way around."

"It seems to me," continued Sharon, "death is never a good deal."

Avalyn listened to her colleagues. She suddenly felt very sad. Was Sherman's decision based on a hope for some personal gain? He seemed to be driven by the notoriety, or perhaps he was acting out of spite. Maybe he had good reason to seek an early death. She knew what he wanted to do and how he planned to do it. But he had not personally told her why, at least not the real reason. She knew what he told the press. But surely there were other options. Why among all his alternatives had he chosen to kill himself? What was his real motivation? Avalyn cupped her hands around her freshly poured cup of coffee and looked at Tabitha, "Do you really think he has nothing left to live for?"

Tabitha shook her head, "Have either of you read his biography?"

Sharon said, "My husband and I watched the movie one night. Nice show, but it was heavily sensationalized. I was on shift the night they brought him in, the real Sherman I mean. I know it was over two decades ago, but I can tell you it was a fairly routine night and would have made for a boring movie."

Tabitha interrupted, "But the book is very good. It goes into detail about his early life. The guy was once a pretty cool guy. He grew up in a small town and moved here to play basketball for the university. After a couple years of college he married a photographer and they had a child, a girl. The book said that the thought of becoming a father opened Joseph's eyes to God. He was baptized in the old Westminster Church shortly before his little girl was born."

Sharon smirked, "Now there's a baptism that didn't take."

Tabitha shook her head, "That's where the book gets

very sad. Sherman's wife had some complications during the delivery and lost her uterus. So the little girl was all they had. The little girl and Sherman were very close. He coached her basketball teams from her elementary years through most of high school. Apparently she was very good, some say on her way to becoming quite the basketball star. Colleges pursued her even during her freshman year of high school. But she died when she was seventeen. She and a friend were walking home after practice one evening when a drunk driver jumped the curb and struck them both from behind. The other girl died at the scene. Sherman's girl was in intensive care for several weeks. She never regained consciousness. The story is very sad. I feel like crying every time I think about it. Sherman had to make the decision to withdraw life support. Can you imagine? Hearing a doctor say your little girl is brain dead and then having to sign a form saying they can pull the plug. The book said Sherman was never the same. His wife blamed him for their daughter's death. The man who hit her only got seven years in prison, half of it suspended if he completed an alcohol rehab program. Not long after that, Sherman's wife fell into a relationship with another man, some guy who worked for Sherman. She divorced Sherman and moved out of state with the other guy. Sherman fell off the grid for a while. His construction company went bankrupt. He just walked away from everything. Then years later, he walked into a police station and turned himself in. He 'fessed up to several unsolved murders including the suspicious death of the man who had killed his daughter."

Tabitha was interrupted by a light knock at the door. The three women became suddenly silent. They gave each other puzzled glances, perplexed about who would knock on the door of the break room. The door was never locked. The area was open for staff. Why would anyone knock?

Avalyn broke the silence, "Door's open. Come in."

The door opened slowly. An extended high pitched squeak resonating from a hinge added to the momentary suspense. Each woman pivoted in her chair to face the opening door.

Then as if sneaking into the room, Chaplain Moffat peered around the door. A childlike smile spread across his face. "Well, hello friends. It appears as though I've been caught in the act."

Sharon leaned back and crossed her arms, "Caught in the act of mischief or ministry?"

The chaplain stepped through the door and held up both hands as if to indicate surrender. In his right hand he held a paper bag containing an item of enough mass to cause the floor of the sack to sag slightly, "I assure you my intentions are pure. However, I am afraid my opportunity for secrecy has passed, and I have failed in preventing the left hand from seeing the actions of the right."

Tabitha clapped her hands together and spoke in a flirtatious tone, "Oh, a secret. Tell us Chaplain. What is your secret?"

The chaplain extended his arm and placed the paper sack on the table. Avalyn gave him a wary smile. She reached into the sack and pulled out a bag of freshly ground coffee beans; the women instantly responded with genuine laughter, the kind of laugh that expresses unexpected joy.

Sharon reached for the bag, "Wow. This is the good stuff. Is this a bribe? I accept. You may have my job for the rest of the day."

Avalyn looked up, "So, Chaplain, what is the occasion?"

"Well, I wish I could say my purposes were nobler, but I merely intended to sneak in and brew a pot of coffee. The coffee maker in our office is broken. I don't mean to interrupt."

Sharon pointed across the table, "Tabitha there has beaten you to the brew. She's our jail-house barista, you know, a real coffee connoisseur. She just made a pot. Good stuff, too. Just grab yourself a cup."

Chaplain Moffat poured a cup of coffee and stood at the table for a moment. His very presence induced an awkward silence among the typically talkative nurses. The chaplain motioned to the television screen, "So, it appears that we are about to get our fifteen minutes of fame."

A news break flashed across the television screen showing a reporter who stood before a backdrop of the prison; a marquee-style headline extended across the bottom of the screen announcing a prison inmate planned to take advantage of the Death with Dignity Act. Poster-wielding demonstrators could be seen clustered around the prison entrance.

The camera zoomed out to show the reporter was

interviewing Doctor Brant. Both of them stood near the entrance to the prison with demonstrators in the background. Avalyn reached for the remote and turned up the volume, "Looks like our good doctor found the spotlight."

The nurses at the table turned to watch the interview. They did not hear the reporter's first question, but their personal knowledge of the events made the coverage easy enough to follow. Regarding end-of-life issues, Doctor Brant had been identified by the news outlet as an expert, in the loose sense that journalists define experts.

When Avalyn turned up the volume, the screen split between two individuals. Doctor Brant was in one panel of the screen still standing in front of the prison; the other panel showed a religious-appearing individual in clerical garb sitting in what appeared to be an office or library. The reporter engaged them both in two or three minutes of questions about the inmate, Mr. Joseph Sherman, who, in the reporter's words, had "gone public" with his decision to terminate his life.

At one point in the interview, Doctor Brant looked into the camera as if speaking to a personal friend and urged support of what he called Sherman's moral cause, "Make no mistake; we are not talking about suicide. This is a choice being made by a competent, though very ill person while he still has control. There is no dignity in prolonging suffering. Inmates, like all of us, have rights. Rights are conferred by the people. The people of our state have stated clearly that a terminally ill person has the right to choose the time of his or her death. A prisoner may lose certain rights, but the right to die with dignity is not one of them."

Avalyn heard the doctor's words, this time from the impersonal vantage of an outside observer. This gave her time to ponder the issue as one listening at a distance. What he was saying made sense to her, but something about seeing the doctor perform so well on camera irritated Avalyn. She was sympathetic to the doctor's underlying message, but she was frankly offended by his grab for recognition at the expense of an inmate, for whose sensational death he would be the proximate, though absent cause.

Avalyn muted the television. She turned toward Chaplain Moffat, "Tell us Chaplain, what do you think of suicide? Is it unforgiveable?"

In any other polite company, the question may have seemed rude or out of place. But if Chaplain Moffat was surprised or in any way offended by the abrupt question, he did not show it. He enjoyed answering questions, or more specifically, answering people. And when answering people, the chaplain had a unique way of dissecting a question to determine the real request.

Chaplain Moffat took a calm sip of coffee and returned the question, "What is your belief, my dear?"

The other nurses looked at Avalyn. She was not accustomed to sharing her beliefs, at least not in public. But she craved trustworthy guidance. So Avalyn took a thoughtful breath and answered, "When I was a teenager, I heard a minister say that suicide was self-murder, a personal offense against God. I guess it never really made sense to me. How could a loving God, or even a vengeful God for that matter, condemn a person, who, in a moment of despair seeks release from suffering?"

"Do you believe he spoke the truth?"

"I think he meant well. He was a loving man. We were just teenagers in the uncertain throes of adolescence. He probably just intended to scare us away from killing ourselves."

Sharon interjected, "He was right; suicide is such a painful affair."

The chaplain rubbed his chin and looked up as if thinking, "I wonder if it is fair to say that not all suicides are equal."

The three nurses reared up, caught unexpectedly off guard by the chaplain's comment. Tabitha articulated what they were each thinking, "Do you think suicide could be good?"

The chaplain took another sip of coffee and smiled, "Well, perhaps. Can you think of cases where the voluntary act of taking one's own life is considered good?"

Tabitha nodded, "Maybe when a person dies to protect someone else, like a fireman running into a burning building or a soldier who throws himself onto a grenade to save his fellow soldiers?"

"Ah, now that's a good point. Sacrificial death is highly esteemed."

Avalyn raised both eyebrows. She articulated her next question at a slow, thoughtful pace, "So let's say a person with a costly terminal illness voluntarily terminates his or her life in order to prevent a burden falling to his or her family. Would that count as a sacrificial death?"

The chaplain nodded, "Perhaps, but that's dangerous territory. Are we willing to take that to its logical conclusion and say that a person who is a burden to his or her family has a duty to die? Or, would you say that an individual has an obligation to end his or her life when a prolonged illness becomes an emotional, psychological, or social burden to others?"

Avalyn shook her head, "I would not personally go that far, no. But surely there are cases where suicide is morally permissible for a terminally ill person, assuming it is voluntary with no compulsion."

The chaplain answered, "Well if a person believes, as many moderns believe, that the greatest good in life is to maximize pleasure and minimize pain, then yes, I would have to concede that suicide in cases that prevent future pain, whether to oneself or others, would be considered a virtue, an act that maximizes the good."

Sharon raised a skeptical eyebrow, "But you don't really believe that, do you?"

"I believe it is misguided. Maximizing pleasure is certainly good; it's just not the greatest good. Minimizing pain is also good; yet, again, it is not the greatest good."

Tabitha sat on her hands and spoke in an almost giddy voice, "Alright, so what is the greatest good?"

The chaplain smiled, "Ah, I've been around a long time and rarely have I met people willing to ask that most important of questions. Not only are you a connoisseur of coffee, I should think you are also a connoisseur of wisdom; for among the greatest philosophers, anyone who pursues an answer to the question of the greatest good truly has a love for wisdom. But let's not get distracted. We first want to know what happens to a person who believes that personal physical or mental satisfaction is the greatest good. How would you describe such a person?"

Avalyn looked puzzled and answered slowly with a rise in her voice, more indicative of a question than an answer, "I would say he or she is healthy?"

"What do you mean by healthy?"

"I mean the person is able to enjoy life, you know, not just living, but living well."

"And does living well imply any obligation to the well-being of other people?"

"I'm not sure I understand your question."

"Well, if an individual enjoys a fulfilling life, but that life harms or oppresses others, would you still call it living well?"

"Can you give us an example?"

"Sure. Let me think." The chaplain rubbed his chin, first looking upward, then as if piecing together a recent memory he said, "Do you remember the news reports about the executive who was arrested for forcing foreign, kidnapped women into slave labor on his estate? He was content. But his personal satisfaction was founded on the oppression of others. Would you say his life was good?"

Sharon smirked, "Good for him, maybe."

"But good in the broad sense, as opposed to evil?" asked the chaplain.

Avalyn crossed her arms as if to feign offense at the question, "Of course not."

"Forgive me. I know that was a ridiculous question, and I know none of you support human trafficking. But what do you think keeps most people from doing such things?"

Sharon answered, "I would say that is why we have laws?"

"Exactly. I agree. But the law does not actually prevent people from harming others. I mean the written words themselves; they do not change a person's behavior. That's why we have higher authorities, such as law enforcement. Would you agree?"

The nurses nodded in unison as Avalyn answered, "Yes, of course."

"Now think about what happens when an individual becomes so morally myopic so as to believe that the greatest good is to fulfill only his or her personal desires without regard for others or a higher authority."

Tabitha rolled her eyes, "Sounds like a few of our customers."

"I think so. That is the essence of criminal thinking, is it not? We know exactly where that type of thinking leads. The result is vice, not virtue."

Avalyn looked upward, searching for the meaning behind the chaplain's thoughts, "So are you suggesting voluntary termination of life is a selfish act, or worse, a criminal act?"

"Absolutely not. Please do not mistake my comments for such an error. I can think of many reasons a person may end his or her life, most of them very sad and a few of them perhaps noble. I'm only pointing out that people who truly believe that the greatest good is found in maximizing pleasure or minimizing pain are misguided and more likely to fall for a lie that suicide somehow achieves a good goal. But suicide should not be claimed as good or beautiful or any of the other silly euphemistic terms people like to use to describe it. In the end it…"

Suddenly the door to the break room swung open. The chaplain stopped his thought, interrupted midsentence by an additional visitor to the break room.

The group looked toward the door. An officer partially leaned in. He looked directly at each of the nurses in turn as if trying to identify someone. When he locked eyes with Avalyn he said, "Excuse me ladies, the Superintendent would like to see Nurse Robbins in his office."

"Now?"

"Absolutely. The Wall does not know the word 'later.'"

CHAPTER NINE

THE WALL

"We have a situation. Mr. Joseph Sherman has told the world he wishes to end his life today. Just end it all right here in prison."

- Antonio Washington
Superintendent

Avalyn stood outside the superintendent's office. Her palms became moist, and she felt beads of sweat forming on her forehead. Closed door meetings in the superintendent's office typically meant trouble. Why did this feel like being called to the principal's office? She was not prepared for a confrontation. Perhaps the superintendent only needed information about the suicide attempt that morning, or maybe he had questions about Sherman's decision to terminate his life. She gently knocked on the door. There was no response, so she turned the handle and opened the door just a crack.

The superintendent, a man named Antonio Washington, was seated at his desk. He was an imposing gentleman, broad and tall, with tightly trimmed, curly, grey-streaked hair lending a certain air of dignity to his otherwise rough appearance. In his younger years, he played as a linebacker for three different professional football teams. He served mostly in back-up training roles, but if you were to meet the man unexpectedly, you would recognize the feeling no doubt experienced by more than a few running backs who rounded the corner on a football field only to meet his impenetrable frame. Fellow players called him "The Wall," a term still used by prison inmates and officers. Nothing happened in the prison without first facing the scrutiny of this fortress of a man.

Avalyn locked eyes with Superintendent Washington who was holding a telephone to his ear. He made a waving motion with his opposite hand to bid her into the room.

Avalyn opened the door quietly. As she stepped into the office, she was silently greeted by three other people sitting at a small conference table on the backside of the office. Avalyn knew two of them. Lieutenant John Burke sat to the left wearing his crisply ironed white uniform shirt and navy tie held in place by a gold plated tie tack. He paused from writing something in his flip-style notebook and raised his eyebrows at Avalyn to acknowledge her arrival.

Sitting next to him was the state's pharmacist, Cynthia Osterman, a petite, anxious-appearing woman in casual attire who had the pale complexion of someone whose work involved far too many hours separated from meaningful sun exposure. She nervously smiled at Avalyn.

Next to these two was a sharply dressed man in a well-tailored suit jotting notes on a legal pad. An opened briefcase full of documents was on the table in front of him.

Superintendent Washington completed his call with a sharp single phrase, "Absolutely, Governor, it is understood."

He hung up the phone, and standing from his chair, welcomed Avalyn to the table, "Nurse Robbins, I think you know Lieutenant Burke and Doctor Osterman. Let me introduce you to Mr. John Templin. He is the state's attorney general."

Mr. Templin removed his reading glasses and greeted Avalyn. She returned the greeting and took the open seat. She noticed Cynthia nervously tapping her hand on a small, black, unmarked container while the lieutenant held his hands folded on the table in front of him as if in seated attention.

Superintendent Washington pointed out his window overlooking the crowd of demonstrators in front of the prison. He did not soften his words, "We have a situation. Mr. Joseph Sherman has told the world he wishes to end his life today. Just end it all right here in prison. Apparently it is legal for him to do so. But what is not clear to me is how this can happen. How does a man housed in a secure medical infirmary with a private medical condition get exclusive exposure in the media? And who has given the inmate the authority to kill himself? I certainly did not authorize anyone to kill himself in this facility. And now Doctor Osterman shows up in my house with a package of deadly drugs to give this man. I understand why they keep medical and security in separate divisions, but don't you think matters of this magnitude should be cleared by this office? "

Cynthia's eyes widened. She interrupted apologetically, "Sir, I'm only filling a prescription given to me by Doctor Brant."

"I understand that, but if Doctor Brant told you to deliver a handgun to an inmate who wanted to terminate his life, I hope by all that is holy that you would refrain from entering this facility with a firearm."

Cynthia placed her hand on the case in her lap, "These

are pills, sir, not a gun."

"But a deadly dose of pills, I presume?"

"Yes, the dosage is lethal."

"Then you see my problem. I absolutely cannot allow a lethal weapon through these doors."

The superintendent looked at Avalyn, "What does this guy have? Cancer or something?"

Up until now Avalyn had remained respectfully silent. She smiled cordially, "Forgive me, Superintendent, I cannot discuss private health information without written consent from the patient."

"Private? The good doctor is all over the news telling people he is the first in the state to provide a prisoner with an assisted death. And it is happening under my roof. I think we are far past concerns for privacy. What am I to do?"

"Don't allow it sir; the risk to the security of the facility is too high," said the lieutenant.

The attorney cleared his throat, "The inmate won a court order to receive this treatment."

"So let him sue us; inmates do it all the time. We will appeal to higher courts. Let them find a better solution. This is my facility. I refuse to allow an inmate to dictate the terms of his incarceration. What's going to happen when every inmate with an ingrown toenail decides it is better to die than to serve a sentence?" Superintendent Washington pointed toward the phone on his desk, "The governor is demanding an answer. He wants to release a statement to reassure the public."

Lieutenant Burke asked, "What does the law say?"

All eyes turned to the attorney. Mr. Templin replaced his reading glasses and pulled a document from his briefcase, "Put simply, any adult citizen of the state with a terminal illness reasonably determined to cause death in six months or less may voluntarily request and consume a lethal prescription of medication intended to end his or her life without fear of legal repercussions."

"Please tell me inmates are not eligible," stated Lieutenant Burke.

Mr. Templin removed his glasses, "Inmates retain the right to whatever standard of health care is generally expected in the community."

Superintendent Washington slapped his open hand on the table, "This is not health care; it's death care. We already have a hospice program. Inmates get excellent end-of-life care. I refuse to let inmates kill themselves and turn this institution into a death center. Can you imagine the accusations? Surely we can refuse to participate as a matter of conscience?"

"The law does include a conscience clause for physicians who decline to participate."

"So have Doctor Brant opt out."

Cynthia pushed the small case across the table, "It's too late for that. He has already written the prescription. This is what he ordered."

The others reflexively leaned back slightly in response to seeing the container on the table. Superintendent Washington looked at the small, flat case. His eyebrows lowered over his deep set eyes in a focused gaze, "Show us the medication."

Cynthia opened the case to reveal three blister packs with thirty capsules per card packaged under individual clear plastic bubbles. She held up the packs as if she were revealing three oversized playing cards showing them to the superintendent. In the top right corner of each card was a printed sticker with the name JOSEPH SHERMAN along with a birthdate, prisoner identification number, and drug information.

"What is the drug?" asked the Superintendent.

"It's called secobarbital."

"I see that. But what kind of drug is it? I mean what does it do?"

"It's a barbiturate; basically a strong sedative."

"How many does it take to, uh, you know, do the job, so to speak?"

"Normally anesthesiologists would administer from one to three for light sedation, such as before surgery."

"No, I mean how many does a person take for euthanasia?"

"All of them. There are ninety pills here, thirty in each pack."

The Lieutenant pointed to the packs, "Forgive my ignorance here; are you saying a person must swallow all those pills at once?"

Cynthia laughed nervously. Her voice took on a higher pitch, "No, the capsules must be emptied. The patient is supposed to open each of the capsules and pour the powder into a drink, like fruit juice or something, then swallow the entire solution over about ten minutes. They say trying to take that many capsules at once raises the risk that the medication may be absorbed in the stomach at different rates. The recommendation is to dissolve the powder from the capsules in liquid so that it can be consumed all at once."

The Superintendent raised his eyes to the ceiling, "This is just getting worse. We're talking about letting inmates drink the Kool-Aid."

The lieutenant spoke up, "You said these are just sleeping pills, like a sedative?"

"Yes."

The Lieutenant touched his fingertips to his lips as if in thought, "Superintendent, I have to advise you not to allow this substance into the prison. It's too risky. A substance like this, if diverted, can cause serious harm and threaten the security of the institution. Our duty is first and foremost to the safety of inmates and the public."

"Lieutenant Burke is correct. Does the law allow us to opt out as an institution?"

Mr. Templin nodded, "Institutions may, as a matter of policy, restrict employees from participating."

Washington slammed his hand down on the table again, "There you go. As a matter of policy, this medication will not be allowed in the institution."

"I'm afraid it's not that easy," said Mr. Templin as he thumbed through additional documents he had pulled from his briefcase. He stopped and held his finger over a line from an article, an opinion piece of some sort, "If you restrict inmates from participation, you will place yourself and the department at significant legal risk, not to mention political risk."

"Please explain yourself."

"Well, unlike a person in the general public, an inmate cannot just choose an alternate doctor in cases where his or her doctor declines to participate. Inmates have no choice in physicians. Refusing to give Mr. Sherman his prescribed medication could be interpreted as a violation of his Eighth Amendment rights. Federal courts consistently rule in favor of inmates in these cases. Forcing an individual to suffer through a terminal illness is seen as a form of cruel and unusual punishment. Furthermore, let me remind you that the sponsor of this law is the chairman of the senate finance committee. That committee holds the purse strings over this department."

The lieutenant sighed in disgust, "Why does it sound like this criminal has put us in our own handcuffs?"

"I can think of more crass analogies," replied the attorney. "If you refuse this inmate's requests, you can basically hand him a blank check, and you can be sure our esteemed senator will make sure every penny comes out of your departmental pocket."

Superintendent Washington folded his arms, not to be mistaken for a sign of resignation, "Ok, let's say for the sake of argument that we have no choice but to let this thing happen. What other options do we have? Can we release him on parole?"

"Not likely. He is in for life without eligibility for parole. And the parole board does not meet for another three weeks."

The Superintendent gave a single, snarky laugh, "So according to this death law an inmate can just skip the whole parole process. No hearing. No weighing of the public impact. I mean at a parole hearing they would at least take into account the inmate's crimes and the interests of the victims or the victims' families. But now we're saying that if an inmate gets really sick, he can just check out early. No parole. No review. No concern for the law or the process. How is this just?"

The lieutenant asked, "Would he be eligible for a special medical parole?"

"To be eligible for a medical parole he cannot be capable of recommitting the crimes for which he is incarcerated," answered the attorney.

The lieutenant turned toward Avalyn, "The guy is terminal right?"

Avalyn felt a flush of heat rising into her neck and face as if under some unseen spotlight. She knew the answer was not what her colleagues wanted to hear. The thought of getting Sherman out of prison was enticing. All they had to do was report to the parole board that Sherman was very sick and unable to commit crimes any longer. That would be a lie, of course; Sherman was sick, but he was not incapacitated, not yet anyway. For a moment Avalyn weighed the ramifications of living with a lie. Surely a lie on her conscience would be more tolerable than living with a man's death. In the end however, truth trumped temptation, and Avalyn answered with candid honesty, "Mr. Sherman has a serious diagnosis, this is true. However, this just means he will die sometime in the next six months. Maybe sooner. Maybe later. He actually looks healthy right now. He's losing weight and having a little trouble swallowing, but he still exercises and reads books and irritates the staff."

The attorney interrupted, "The idea behind the Death with Dignity Law is that a person may end his life privately on his own terms before an illness progresses. I'm afraid that once the inmate reaches the point at which he is eligible for parole, he would not be capable of taking the drugs."

"So if he takes the medication in private while in the infirmary, will that compromise anyone's safety?" asked the Superintendent.

"Not if he takes the drug at the time it's given to him. But what if he does not take it immediately? What if he hoards it or uses it one pill at a time for a sedative or tries to sell the pills?" asked the lieutenant.

The Superintendent turned to Avalyn, "Nurse Robbins, how do you feel about preparing and administering the solution to Mr. Sherman?"

Avalyn's eyes fell, "It's my job, sir. I would be untruthful if I said I agreed with his decision or that I cherish the thought of participating in his death. I suppose in the end, I have a duty to render care…"

The attorney did not allow her to finish, "I'm sorry to interrupt; the nurse cannot prepare the solution. The law is clear that only the patient may prepare the drug and then self-administer the drug at a time of his choosing. No other person may assist. This must remain an individual act from start to finish. The inmate must prepare his own solution."

"Why can't our pharmacist prepare it ahead of time?"

Cynthia shook her head. She shoved the medication cards across the table toward Avalyn. Her voice trembled, "You are talking about an off label use of a pharmaceutical agent. I will not compromise my license by compounding a deadly drug. I am only here to deliver a prescribed medication to the medical department. How it is distributed is up to you. I want no further part of this."

Superintendent Washington wiped his hands together, "So be it. I wash my hands of the whole thing. The courts have ordered a medication be given to an inmate. This is between the courts and the medical department. My officers will not participate. But if even one pill is diverted, the whole amount will be confiscated. If he misuses the pills, he loses his right to access them ever again. Are we in agreement?"

The lieutenant shook his head, "I still must protest, sir. He is in a camera cell. Watching a death on a monitor without the ability or authorization to stop the action could be emotionally devastating to our officers."

"I see," said Washington. "Can we turn off the camera in his cell and continue routine visual checks?"

"Yes, sir. If we must."

"And would this protect our legal interests in running the institution?"

Mr. Templin placed his glasses on the table, "I believe that would balance his right to privacy with the department's obligation to maintain the safety of the institution. Yes."

Superintendent Washington shook his head in

frustration at the morbid conclusion to which the group had arrived. He placed both palms on the table and pushed himself into an imposing standing position. He pointed a single raised finger at Cynthia and Avalyn, "I want to make it very clear. I oppose this action. The court may have ordered this, but I refuse to bear the weight of responsibility. If you give him that medication, I cannot protect you; I will not protect you from the ramifications."

Avalyn looked at the packets in front of her. She did not respond immediately. She felt sad. The image of justice standing blindfolded with balance in hand flashed through her mind. How appropriate, she thought. Judges in this case had applied a law blindly, not out of impartial fairness, but with a blind unwillingness to foresee the unintended injustices imposed by the new law. Don't people know that a death affects caregivers as much as anyone else? How much more if the one charged with giving care is asked to participate in the cause of death? She thought about how this medication was not some antibiotic meant to cure a deadly disease. The patient was not taking this to cure an infection or to treat some discomfort. This medication was intended to be taken only once. It was not treatment; it was an exit. The effects were intended to be final and permanent. There are no refills or second doses. The capsules in front of her took on an almost metaphysical quality, ninety little demons hungry for access to a hopeless soul; or were they angels sent to escort a redeemed soul into eternal life? She felt the eyes of the room focused on her. Finally she looked up at the superintendent, "I will give him the medications as ordered, but please do not ask me to do this alone."

The superintendent's expression remained serious. He held a hand out toward the door indicating the meeting was adjourned, "Security for my staff, including you, Nurse Robbins, will remain my first priority. But to the extent you elect to proceed with providing these pills to Mr. Sherman, the medical department stands alone on this decision. It cannot be otherwise."

Avalyn slid three medication cards into the carrying case and departed the superintendent's office. Lieutenant Burke escorted her back to the infirmary. Both of them walked in foreboding silence as magnetic locks banged and barred corridor barriers slid open before them.

When they reached the infirmary, the lieutenant said, "Goodbye, ma'am. And for what it's worth, I do not envy your task."

CHAPTER TEN

DEFINING A DIGNIFIED DEATH

"I am very skeptical of people who say that self-killing lends dignity to a person's death. It seems to me that we may honor a person without esteeming the person's manner of death."

- Robert Moffat, M.Th.
Prison Chaplain

Avalyn watched the lieutenant proceed down the corridor. Then she entered the infirmary and stood quietly for a moment in front of the medication room. The case in her hands took on a surreal heaviness, as if the weight of each capsule were mysteriously increasing. This physical sensation was matched by an emotional heaviness as she began to feel the weight of her task. The welling mix of melancholy and distress produced a solitary tear which, once fully formed, slid down the curve of her cheek.

A familiar voice called out from behind her, "You need my help, Nurse Robbins?"

"No, Officer Vatel, thank you. Pharmacy just delivered these medications for the inmates. I'll be right out."

Avalyn swiped a special key card and entered the medication room. Once inside, she used a standard metal key hanging around her neck to access a separate narcotic safe. She placed the three blister cards neatly within the locked case.

After depositing the medication, Avalyn took a few moments to regain her composure, and then she returned to the nurses' desk. From there she called to Vatel, who was walking around the infirmary in a routine afternoon count peering into each cell, "How are our patients?"

"Better with you here, Nurse Robbins," Vatel

motioned toward a cell behind him, "The chaplain is in with Mr. Sherman."

Avalyn looked over Vatel's shoulder toward cell number twelve. Through the cell window she could see the chaplain sitting at Joseph Sherman's bedside. Though she could not hear their voices, she could see body language consistent with laughter, an altogether unexpected scene in the closing hours of a man's life. *A man's final visit with a holy cleric should be more serene*, she thought.

An inmate from the kitchen staff entered through the back door pushing a large silver cart containing stacks of plastic lunch trays. Vatel greeted the kitchen worker and walked ahead of him systematically opening each cell, one cell at a time, long enough for the food service inmate to deliver a meal to each patient.

Avalyn's thoughts suddenly turned to home. She looked at her watch. *It's lunch time at home as well.* She imagined her children sitting in a high chair and a booster seat at the kitchen table, their tiny mouths smeared with peanut butter and fruity goo licked from jelly-laden fingers. She smiled at the thought of her hero making funny bubble noises with a straw in the children's milk, and she could hear their giggles in her mind.

She looked around the infirmary. The inmates' attention had turned to food and this culinary diversion afforded Avalyn a brief, much-needed moment to check in with her husband, so she reached for the phone on her desk and dialed home.

She cupped her hand over the receiver and whispered

cryptic, albeit endearing, phrases, "Hi, Babe. I just needed to hear your voice. Yes, I am fine. It's just one of those days. I'll tell you about it tonight. How are the kids?"

At one point, she smiled and began talking to one of her children. Her voice took on the altered tone of a proud parent speaking to a pre-schooler, "Hello, my prince. What are you doing today? Wow, a dinosaur, really? I can't wait to see it. You are a very good painter. Well, soon. Mommy's taking care of sick people today. I'll be home tonight. Help daddy protect Sissy, ok? I'm proud of you."

She spoke again with her husband. The conversation was routine, and to an outside observer the topics would seem mundane. But for the two of them, the short conversation had deep meaning. It reminded Avalyn of bygone days when briefly, if only in passing, they could share time together at work. For the moment, it felt like he was standing right beside her. Her body relaxed as the burdens of the day faded, and for an instant, she felt safe, untouchable even.

Then she heard Joseph Sherman's cell door being opened. She looked up to see Chaplain Moffat walking out of Sherman's cell, so she whispered into the phone, "I've got to go. Love you." And she hung up.

Suddenly she felt a band-like tightness returning to her chest. The chaplain approached Avalyn at the nurses' computer. He leaned forward over the desk and whispered, "Excuse me, Nurse Robbins. Mr. Sherman asked me to let you know he wishes to proceed."

Avalyn looked back at the chaplain. She felt an

uncomfortable lump in her throat as if her conscience were a physical knot, tied halfway between her head and her heart, pulled in both directions in some moral tug-of-war. Maybe she still had time to back out. She looked both ways, as if to make sure the area was clear, then she inquired, "Chaplain, may I ask a personal question?"

"Of course, my dear."

"Do you agree with Mr. Sherman's decision? I mean, is he right to seek his own death?"

Chaplain Moffat looked at Avalyn with respectful warmth. He breathed deeply and said, "I cannot comment on the morality of his choice, but I do believe a man actively seeking to end his life deserves our prayers as much as a man who chooses to die naturally."

Avalyn nodded. She understood the Chaplain's need for discretion, but she was not satisfied with his answer.

Chaplain Moffat noted Avalyn's frustration. He bent forward to make eye contact with her, and then speaking softly asked, "May I go out on a limb and presume that your question is not about Mr. Sherman?"

Avalyn responded with a shy grin, "You understand people well. May I speak with you in private?"

"My time is yours. Where shall we talk?"

True privacy is largely non-existent in the prison. The only strictly off-camera areas are inside staff restrooms and in senior staff office suites. Exam rooms in the medical clinic, however, are semi-private, on camera but without intercoms.

Avalyn recommended moving to an empty trauma room where at least the conversation could be out of sight from inmates.

The chaplain followed Avalyn through the infirmary into an oversized, clinic-style emergency room with a single, wheeled gurney and an overhead swinging surgical lamp. Open-faced cabinets hung on the walls of the room, in which neatly organized medical supplies could be seen. Three valves protruded from the back wall of the room, labelled for oxygen, air, and suction. Next to the gurney was a portable bedside toilet.

Avalyn entered the trauma bay and jumped up onto the center of the gurney, sitting with her legs hanging off the side.

Chaplain Moffat looked around the room. The only remaining place to sit was on the bedside commode. He smiled and lowered the commode lid, "May I take the seat of honor?"

Avalyn blushed, "I'm so sorry, Chaplain. Would you prefer to sit here on the gurney?"

"Not at all, my dear. Now tell me, what is on your mind?"

Avalyn took a deep breath. She gripped the cushion beneath her, "Chaplain, I've been thinking about what you said earlier. And I wonder how you feel about helping a terminally ill person die, I mean actually helping them, you know, do it."

The chaplain nodded without immediately answering. He looked into Avalyn's eyes with a depth of compassion that communicated that he heard the question, and even more, that he could see that something troubled her to the core.

Then he said thoughtfully, "You have an amazing job, Avalyn."

"How do you mean?"

"Well, you are an advocate and true caregiver for this motley group of offenders that most would say is undesirable at best. But it strikes me just now that yours is one of the few professions that has something priceless to offer even the most malicious individual in the closing moments of his life."

Avalyn tilted her head and squinted as if to physically underline her question, "What do you think I have to offer?"

"Why, the touch of another human being, of course. More to the point, the touch of a nurse. I'm no doctor, but I don't know of any palliative medication that compares to the caring touch of an attentive nurse. So when you ask me how I feel about helping a person pass from this life, I am suddenly taken with a sense of awe that you are one of the few people who are invited into those sacred moments that surround the end of life."

Avalyn returned a thankful smile, "You give me too much credit, Chaplain. I'm not prepared to play this role. I was unexpectedly dragged into this by a scheduling game of chance. Today just happened to be my lucky shift."

"You are a brave woman. I'm amazed at your ability to bear such a load with professional poise."

Avalyn leaned forward, "Chaplain, I need someone to help me think this through. Am I doing the right thing as a professional by helping a man die with dignity?"

The chaplain looked over the top of his glasses at Avalyn, "Do you believe death threatens the dignity of dying people?"

"Not death itself, but the process maybe."

"What does dying with dignity mean to you?"

"I guess I would say it means a person is able to die at a time and place and in a manner that is right for him or her. I don't think it would mean the same thing for everyone; it is such a personal decision."

"I see," said the chaplain. Then he looked upward thoughtfully, "So to lose autonomy and privacy at one's death would be undignified?"

"Yes, I suppose so."

"Well, I think you are correct in most respects. On our death bed we are most vulnerable and so completely dependent on others. When else in life is our dignity so threatened? But, would you say that *only* the terminally ill have a right to autonomy and privacy in matters of life and death?

"No, I feel everyone deserves the right to make personal, private decisions."

"So I wonder if it would be reasonable to open the right to die to everyone regardless of age or disability."

"Don't you think that's a little extreme?"

"Not extreme; I'm just trying to be consistent. Some people get the idea that the ill, the elderly, and the mentally distressed have less dignity in the closing days of life than the young, strong, and clear-minded. Is compassion something to be rationed? It seems to me that if suicide is a cure for all that is undignified, the treatment should be available to everyone who finds himself in an undignified situation, regardless of the anticipated duration of life."

"Well, if that's the case then I would say no; maybe it's inconsistent, but I feel there is a big difference between a young person who is depressed and a person who is terminally ill. I mean one may not see a way out, but for a person about to die there really is no way out."

"So if a patient asks you for help in dying, how do you determine the difference?"

Avalyn held both hands upward in resignation, "Well, that's my problem. I can't really tell. I can't see a person's motivation. There's no truth detector for me to verify a person's reason for seeking to die. My training tells me to do everything possible to stop a suicide. We put people on suicide precautions, place them in camera cells, and refer them for counseling. But when a person is truly ill, I mean at death's door, it seems like stopping the process is just artificially prolonging suffering."

The chaplain shifted toward the front of his seat and gripped his hands together. His face momentarily glowed like a teenage boy telling a friend about a special girl. "May I tell you a personal story?"

"Of course."

"It's about my wife, the only woman I ever loved. I had to say good-bye to her about six years ago, not long before you started working here, as I think of it now. She was an amazing human being who lived to the age of seventy-four. Her mind and, for the most part, her body remained strong until the end. She was an elementary school teacher who loved her students as if they were her own children. We were unable to have children of our own. Her students and their families became our extended family. For so many years she provided attentive care for those kids, especially those who were hard to love. Even in retirement she would visit the school and ask which kids were struggling; that's who she would tutor, sometimes sitting patiently with those kids for hours. And she loved to write. She penned many inspirational short stories published in various magazines. But I think her best writing took the form of personalized, handwritten letters. Her artistic penmanship, coupled with her moving way with words, made each of her letters an invaluable, personally signed work of art. You'll think me overly sentimental, but I still keep a collection of letters she wrote to me over the years. She was my best friend. A few years ago she died from complications of a stroke. We had some warning. She was bedridden for several months, and the stroke had taken away her ability to speak clearly. Then her heart and kidneys started failing. But she could still write, and in a short note, she expressly declined aggressive life-saving measures. The doctors kept her comfortable. Many friends and not a few of her prior students came by to visit her. But at the end, only I was with her, just the two of us in the room. I sang to her and told her stories about how she affected so many lives. Then on that last day, after several hours of labored breathing, she took a few final struggling breaths, and it was over. The monitor showed her heart slow to a flat line, and she was gone. It was as if I was waving goodbye from the shore as she departed on a voyage. I kissed her goodbye and sat silently in a chair, watching over her body until the men from the funeral home arrived."

"That is beautiful. She sounds like an amazing woman."

"Oh, she was the best part of my every day. So, I suppose that's what I think of when I think of a dignified death. It was peaceful, just the two of us. And my wife's wishes were honored."

"Forgive me if this sounds disrespectful, but may I ask you a question about your wife's passing?"

"Of course."

"Is there something wrong with trying to orchestrate that type of death? I mean setting a time and place to ensure the dignity of the person passing?"

"May I also ask you a question about my wife's death?"

"Sure."

"What do you think lent dignity to the occasion?"

"It sounds like there were a lot of things. The care. The fact that you could be at her side. The chance to say goodbye. She lived a rich life and died peacefully. Who could ask for more?"

"So you noticed it had little, if anything, to do with the manner of her death, only that it was peaceful."

"It sounds like it was ideal."

"What I hope you would see is that my wife was dignified, truly honored, not by her death, but by others, in spite of her death. I am very skeptical of people who say that self-killing lends dignity to a person's death. It seems to me that we may honor a person without esteeming the person's manner of death."

"So I guess that is my struggle. How do we lend dignity to the death of a patient who wants to take his own life?"

"I wish there were a better answer. I really do. But, I do not believe you can."

"Why not?"

"Well, my dear, all human beings enter the world under a sentence of death. We draw our first breath on death row, condemned to die from day one, without eligibility for pardon. Whether the sentence is carried out in one year or a hundred years, it does not matter; the outcome is the same. That is the tragedy of death. No one escapes. No one is immune. Suicide is merely the word we use to describe a person's actively participating in his or her own execution. Suicide is heartbreaking because a person is not only the victim but also the causal agent of his or her death. Perhaps this makes a suicide the darkest of all deaths. But death by suicide is no more evil than any other cause of death. Nor is suicide, even in its more sterile medicalized forms, more dignified than other forms of death. A black marker does not make black any brighter. Death itself is evil. Period. There is nothing dignified about it; it is an ugly transition, bloody and painful as the moment of birth, though absent the subsequent joy for those left in its wake. It is altogether undignified and is always a tragedy; at least from our perspective."

Avalyn raised an eyebrow, "Our perspective?"

"Perhaps what appears to be a tragedy for us can be prized from a different point of view. There's an ancient Jewish saying, 'Precious in the sight of God is the death of His saints.' Apparently death is viewed from the other side as something described as precious. It seems to me that suicide is usually a symptom, the resigned act of an individual or a culture that has lost this hope."

Avalyn relaxed and pulled her legs up onto the gurney wrapping her arms around her knees. She felt for a moment like she was sitting with a favorite teacher or beloved grandfather. She listened intently to each statement, eager to understand and hear more.

Suddenly the sound of distant footsteps in the hallway diverted Avalyn's attention. She raised her hand toward the chaplain and looked toward the door. The footsteps approached quickly, then slowed to a cautious pace, coming finally to a stop outside the trauma room. Avalyn and the chaplain looked at each other and then back at the door. There was a knock but no pause before the door swayed opened.

CHAPTER ELEVEN

THE WAGER

"Don't you think making people suffer through cancer is a bit cruel and unusual? If anything, cancer seems a pretty strong argument against a benevolent, all-powerful creator."

- Blaine Russell
Prison Inmate

An officer dressed in a dark blue uniform stuck his head into the trauma room. He looked at the chaplain and then at Avalyn as if visually checking them off of some mental list. Then he said in a professional, serious tone, "Just the two of you in here? No inmates?"

Avalyn nodded, "Yes, sir. Only the two of us. We won't be long. Is there a problem?"

"No ma'am. No problem. Just conducting count before shift change."

The officer backed out of the room and closed the door. He immediately grabbed a pen from his shirt pocket, clicked it a few times, and scribbled something in his notebook. Then he keyed the radio microphone clipped to his shoulder lapel, "Central control. Rover three. Medical clear. I'm headed to Echo mod for count."

Echo mod, another name for Module E, was the primary housing unit for prison workers. Built on a philosophy of restorative justice, prison planners had designed the Echo module to look like an apartment complex or college dorm with the idea that inmates were less likely to return to prison if preparation for the outside world could begin before the day of release. The Echo mod provided opportunities for inmates to live in a community setting and practice the skills required to hold a steady job.

Echo mod contained four room units with eight private rooms in each unit positioned around a central multipurpose room where inmates socialized and shared meals.

Securing a room in the Echo mod was a hard-earned privilege. The inmates in Echo served in prison jobs that required a high level of trust. Many of them worked as personal caregivers for elderly or physically disabled inmates. The prisoners who made up the custodial staff, maintenance staff, and kitchen staff also lived in Echo.

Echo inmates were given latitude in their day-to-day routine. The rules were simple. Show up for work and keep out of trouble. But often keeping rule number one made keeping rule number two very difficult. Work brought in money. Echo mod workers were among the highest paid in the prison, though the prison had relatively few legitimate ways to spend earned cash. Furthermore, work brought inmates into close contact with contraband. They cleaned the medical wing. They worked heavy machinery. They had regular access to food products, cleaning products, and power tools. For many, the general paucity of impulse control, which led many of them to prison in the first place, in the setting of a virtually endless supply of products that were otherwise hard to come by, proved to be a temptation too great to resist.

So, over the years the Echo mod had become a micro stock exchange of sorts, a place where contraband commodities were bought, sold, and traded to support the overall prison economy. The laws of supply and demand exerted their unchecked influence over the Echo mod. Anything with nicotine or other similarly addictive ingredients cost up to a hundred times the going rate in the free world. Pain medications could be worth their weight in some precious metals. And saving up enough to purchase supplies for making tattoo machines or weapons could take as long as it takes the average person to save up to buy a new car.

Money and contraband flowed freely into and then through the module into other parts of the prison largely unnoticed by corrections officers. In reality, every officer and prison employee knew what was happening, and a few had even been manipulated into participating, but the inmates themselves were very good at hiding the illegal practices from the watchful eye of cameras and officers.

And if Echo mod served as a sort of central stock exchange, the poker table served as its trading floor, the forum in which goods were bought, sold, and traded. Of course, poker was not the only game played. Inmates used many different games of chance to exchange property or cash. During down time in the Echo mod's multipurpose area, inmates remained occupied in seemingly endless games of poker, dice, chess, or standard board games. But it was a version of coin-flipping, called *heads-up*, a quick game of chance profoundly dependent on unique house rules, which served as the centerpiece of Echo mod's underground gambling scene.

Gambling in the prison was illegal. The penalty for being caught exchanging goods in a game of chance was severe. Even the suspicion of illegal gambling could result in the transfer of an inmate to solitary confinement in the segregation unit or an appearance before the disciplinary board for possible prolongation of prison time.

Inmates took precautions. Recreational games for pleasure took place at tables all around a gambling table so that the casual observer would not be able to recognize the difference between legal and illegal games. Most games were set up in dark spots, areas out of the view of security cameras. Lookouts remained posted near the module entrance. These lookouts used a variety of methods to alert others to imminent interruptions.

To further hide gambling activities, the inmates had fashioned seemingly innocuous coin-shaped game pieces that served a similar function to poker chips at a casino. These homemade discs were also used as flipping coins in a game of *heads-up*. The coins were made of toilet tissue solidified into discs with a form of glue made from ingredients taken out of the prison kitchen. Each coin was about the size of a quarter. One side of the paper coin had a number representing the coin's value and the other had an inscription, usually an initial or unique icon that functioned as the artist's signature. By convention, the numbered sides of the coins were called heads. The inscribed side was called tails.

An inmate named Blaine sat down at a table in Echo mod. He was a muscular man in his thirties with flowing hair and square facial features. He slapped his hand down on the table and then lifted it up to reveal two white pills. He looked up across the table at three other inmates and said, "I'm in. What's in the pot?"

One of the other inmates, an older gentleman with a large nose and leather-like black skin looked at Blaine over the top of his reading glasses. He did not speak; he only studied Blaine for a moment and then nodded to the others.

The other inmates placed seemingly random items on the table: a cell phone and an envelope containing several small sheets of paper.

"What are the pills?" asked one of the inmates.

"Pain pills. Hydros," answered Blaine.

"Where you come by those?"

"I'm assigned to the infirmary this week. Slipped it off the med cart during an emergency this morning."

"Right on," exclaimed the other inmate. "You're high risk, dude."

"So, what's in the envelope?"

"Postal tea," the other inmate answered. "The paper's soaked in spice. Just put it in hot water for a drink or smoke it."

The older gentleman, nicknamed Boxer, reached under his waistband and pulled out two paper coins. He placed both coins in the palm of his hand and waved them past each player as he recited the rules, "The game's *heads-up*. Each of you gets a throw. Heads up wins. Tails up loses. Odds is a scratch. Winner of three takes all. Five scratches in a row goes to the house. Agreed?"

The other inmates nodded in unison, "Agreed."

Boxer handed the coins to the first inmate. This inmate folded both coins into his closed hand and shook his hands as if preparing to throw a pair of dice. Then he opened his hand and forcefully clapped his other hand down onto the wrist of the hand containing the coins. This action sent the coins suddenly flipping into the air.

Blaine watched the coins rotate. He leaned forward to get a closer look as the coins landed on the table spinning momentarily and then coming to rest. One coin showed heads, the other tails.

"It's a scratch. One for the house," said Boxer with a partial grin.

Blaine reached forward and lifted the coins into his right hand. He too struck his right wrist with his left palm, which sent the coins overturning in the air. The coins revolved and flipped end over end, falling then bouncing on the table in an elastic collision the sound of which was muffled by the fact that the coins were made of an organic material instead of metal.

All three inmates leaned over the table to see the two coins. Both showed tails.

"No points for Blaine. Next throw," said Boxer.

The next inmate threw a scratch.

Then the third inmate picked up the coins. On his throw the coins both landed with heads up.

"That's a point. One up, two to go for the man in the orange shirt."

The inmates laughed.

Blaine stated the obvious, "Boxer, we're all wearing orange."

Boxer sat up straight taking on the air of a carnival announcer, "That's right folks, step right up. Today everyone's a winner." Then he tossed the coins back to the inmate, "Winner gets another throw."

The inmate's next throw was a pair of tails.

Boxer handed the coins to Blaine.

Before Blaine released the next throw, one of the other inmates asked, "So, you ever see that guy Sherman down in the infirmary?"

"What's that to you?"

"Just curious. I'm on grounds today, and they brought us in early. There's a crowd outside going nuts over that guy. News said he's committing suicide today. You think he'll do it? I mean really take his own life?"

Blaine shook the coins in his hand, "What do I care? I overheard the nurse talking with him about cancer or something. Sounds like a bad way to go otherwise."

"How's it going down? Will they inject him or something?"

Blaine leaned forward and spoke softly, "Word has it they're giving him pills, strong downers."

"Intense, man. Any chance you could swing us a few?"

"Well, I made a deal with him this morning. But if you want in, you'll have to bring more than just cell phones to our next game."

Blaine released the coins in his hand. One tails. One heads.

"House has another," laughed Boxer.

One of the inmates leaned back in his chair and looked up at the ceiling. He took a deep, thoughtful breath before sharing his opinion, "Seems like a stupid way to go, if you asked me."

"What makes you say that?"

"'Cause it's like a double suicide. You kill yourself. And then you stand before the judgment of an almighty God and have to explain why your very last act on Earth was to take your own life. I just don't see how that can end well."

Blaine looked at the other inmate and sneered, "You don't have to fear what does not exist."

Suddenly the table, indeed the entire room became very quiet. In the prison, a man may question the justice system or any human authority. But the Supreme Judge of the cosmos was off limits. The other inmates slid back from the table as if to avoid whatever act of divine punishment awaited Blaine's blasphemous statement. Then one of them scowled and asked, "You don't believe in God?"

Blaine held up both hands as if to indicate he had no score to settle, "Whoa. Back down. I'm no atheist; I've got no personal quarrel with the Almighty. I just think there are many paths. You've got yours. Maybe Sherman has his. I just haven't found mine yet."

"But you say God does not exist?"

"No, let me rephrase. I have no proof one way or the other. And you brought up the guy with cancer. Don't you think making people suffer through cancer is a bit cruel and unusual? If anything, cancer seems a pretty strong argument against a benevolent, all-powerful creator."

"Well I'm not standing next to you on Judgment Day," said one of the other inmates.

Boxer rotated a coin in between his fingers. He

squinted his eyes the way a wise man does when listening to another man's point of view, "So, Blaine, what's your case? Make your statement."

"Well I'm just stating the obvious. If God is all-powerful and all-good, then people would not suffer from diseases like cancer. See, if He is all-good and suffering persists, then He must not be all-powerful, because an all-good God would use His power to rid the world of suffering. And if, on the other hand, He is all-powerful, then He must not be all-good, because an all-powerful God would rid the world of evil if He himself were good. And if God is neither all-good nor all-powerful, why even call him God?"

The inmates in the room turned to look at Boxer. Many migrated from other tables so that a crowd of orange-clad inmates stood around the table drawn by the rising tension between Blaine and Boxer.

Boxer felt the eyes of the room on him, and to all appearances, he invited the attention. He leaned back and crossed his arms, "What if your all-powerful and all-good God will one day annihilate all causes of suffering in the world, but He has not yet done so? What if his omnipotence and benevolence are matched by his patience?"

"Then He is a little late to the party, don't you think?"

"Depends on who's at the party," Boxer responded. Then he smiled, "Seems to me if God did a surprise sweep through Echo to rid the mod of evil, you and I both would have reason to worry. I think most of us appreciate the delay in divine justice."

Blaine pointed at Boxer, "You make your bets old man, and I'll make mine. I'm not going to spend my time worried about shaking hands with Saint Peter."

Boxer laughed deeply. This response was unexpected. The inmates were expecting a physical fight; Boxer found Blaine's response truly humorous.

Then Boxer held up one of his coins and held it out to Blaine, "Anyone can talk, boy. Want to make a real statement? Put your money where your mouth is. Care to make a wager?"

Blaine raised an eyebrow, "What's the bet?"

"Either God is or He is not. Which do you wager? Let us put the matter to a test. I, as one believing in God, will pray for Him to reveal Himself in the flip of this coin. If the coin lands as heads, this will be for us proof that God exists. If it lands on tails, this will be proof to us that God does not exist. You, being the agnostic will say that the flipping of a coin is merely an act of chance. There is equal probability of landing on heads or tails. But I don't think this is what you really believe."

Blaine took the coin, "What's the take?"

Boxer pulled out a pencil and wrote in large letters: I-O-U and an amount. He slid the note to the center of the table. The crowd of inmates leaned forward to see what Boxer had written on the paper.

Blaine slid the paper toward himself. He rotated the note in front of him to see the figure written. The words were clear: ten thousand dollars, all or nothing.

Boxer pointed to the note with a second coin he held in his hand, "If you are willing to concede that God exists, say simply heads. Then if the coin lands on heads, you will win the ten thousand dollars. It is nothing to me. I'm in for life. I have no family. I have more than enough to enjoy my days. But for you, surely this is an attractive offer. I am bribing you to save your soul. Admit God is, and if the coin lands heads, you walk out of the mod a wealthy man."

"What's the catch?"

"There's no catch. If you choose to believe, as I do, and call heads, but the coin lands on tails, then my prayers are clearly to no avail. We will both be proven wrong. We'll just tear up that little promissory note and go about our day. My pride will be rightly tempered and you will have lost nothing."

Boxer continued, "On the other hand, you may choose to remain firm to your assertion that God is not. This will be represented by tails. I will ask no money of you; only your promise to hold to your decision. If you choose to deny the existence of a living God simply say tails. If the coin indeed lands on tails, you win the argument. You retain your pride and walk away knowing you chose correctly. But if you choose tails and the coin lands on heads, you do not get the money. It will stay in my account, for you will have chosen poorly."

Boxer held up the coin as if ready to make the toss, "So which do you choose? Tell me now. Either God is or He is not. Heads or tails?"

Blaine shook his head, "And if I refuse to play?"

"You are already committed. I am about to flip the coin. If you say nothing, then it will mean nothing to you, the same as calling tails. But you will still have placed a wager. For the flip is about to occur, and you only have one chance to weigh in on the game. Now tell me which do you choose? Heads or tails?"

Boxer flipped the coin high into the air.

All heads and all eyes in the room looked up as the disc tumbled end over end. But Blaine initially looked around him. It appeared the entire scene was playing out in slow motion.

Other inmates started yelling, "Pick heads, you fool! Pick heads! You have everything to gain and nothing to lose." Blaine's face lit up, and just before the coin was to hit the floor he opened his mouth to speak his decision.

But before he said a word a loud bang echoed through the mod. An inmate next to the door had dropped a book onto the floor. The dropped item was a signal. An officer was approaching the entrance to the mod.

The inmates scattered to their tables and rooms, grabbing and concealing contraband. Blaine lifted the pills off the table and stuffed them back under his waist band. Boxer remained seated.

The officer entered the mod and yelled, "Count and call for afternoon shift."

Most of the inmates lined up at the door. Blaine also walked forward and took his place in line. He was scheduled to clean the infirmary.

The officer keyed his radio microphone, "Central control. Rover three. Echo mod count is clear. Releasing workers to afternoon shift."

The inmates filed out the door. As Boxer rose from

the table to join the line of departing workers, he reached down and looked at the coin still sitting on the floor beside him. As he picked up the coin he shook his head and said to himself, "Young fool, could have had it all."

CHAPTER TWELVE

WALKING IN THE SHADOW OF DEATH

"You are here in this place and time for a reason. I cannot help thinking that something about Mr. Sherman's life and his decision is meant to have some influence on your own search for what is good."

- Robert Moffat, M.Th.
Prison Chaplain

Avalyn looked back at the chaplain, "Are you suggesting that a loss of hope makes people want to do evil?"

"Not at all, my dear, at least not directly. I would say the loss of hope leads to a loss of the desire to pursue that which is good. To lose hope is to lose the strong sense that we are preparing, or are being prepared, for a world beyond this life, a world where we finally become what we have only in this life practiced becoming."

Avalyn closed her eyes. The thought of a world beyond this life momentarily diverted her attention. *Is it true? How is it that I spend my whole life helping individuals evade something about which I know next to nothing? But even if I had strong feelings one way or the other, would it be wrong to impose my belief on someone else?* She looked to the ceiling again, thoughtfully pondering her predicament, "My question is about what I should rightfully do as a medical professional. I don't think my personal belief or disbelief in an afterlife changes my job description."

The chaplain smiled a gentle loving smile, "What if it does matter? 'Our whole life is affected by whether the soul is mortal or immortal.' So says Pascal, the French philospher. What if he were right?"

Chaplain Moffat then sat up straight and looked around the trauma bay, "I am only an outside observer, but it seems to me that much of your professional training has been spent preparing for some medical emergency for which you believe you should be ready, regardless of whether or not the emergency actually comes to pass. This is true in many areas of life, is it not? Being prepared I mean. From life's many preparations we get virtue. When we say something is virtuous, we simply mean it comes from developing a habit for doing what is good, the opposite of vice, which is the habit of doing evil. Virtue therefore comes from practice, like when you practice your life-saving skills in this room so that when the time comes, you are prepared to do the right thing at the right time with the correct piece of equipment to save a life. In the same way, virtue comes from practicing doing what is right and good, so that when faced with moral dilemma you do the right thing, without a second thought, because that is how you've trained."

Then he raised his hand in an open palm gesture, "So you see, acting on lost hope is not inherently evil, but rationally speaking, a person who has lost hope is more likely to do wrong than do good, including self-killing for perhaps the wrong reasons. I'm not saying a person who has lost hope is evil. I'm merely saying that when a person loses hope of a life beyond this present life, he or she will logically revert just to doing whatever maximizes personal pleasure and minimizes personal pain without reverence toward God or consideration of the lasting effect on others."

Avalyn listened. She allowed the chaplain's words to fill gaps in her own experience, but up until that point the discussion remained peripheral to her real concern. She looked at the chaplain. Her lower lip began to tighten and then quiver. "Chaplain, I have been asked to help Sherman end his life."

Chaplain Moffat leaned back with his arms folded, "Mr. Sherman's request troubles you?"

"Not so much his request. He is a grown man and can ask for whatever he wants. It bothers me that everyone expects me to be the one who gives him the lethal drugs. His choices are his to make, but I don't feel like I am being given a choice."

"And this choice you describe, is it a choice you wish to make?"

"I don't know. It would be easier just to follow orders and let someone else bear the weight of responsibility for the decision. I mean I was given the task of delivering a medication. Surely I am not wrong just to do what I'm told to do. But somehow it just doesn't feel right."

"Well let's think about that. You realize that millions of people were killed in the world's great atrocities by average men and women, many of them highly educated, who were simply doing what they had been told to do. The American Trail of Tears, the Armenian genocide, the Jewish holocaust, the Cambodian killing fields, bloodshed in Rwanda, ethnic cleansing in Bosnia, and genocide in Darfur all have this one thing in common: the most inhumane acts of violence were committed not by the monsters who led the people, but by the average people who were just following orders. I suppose that is an unfortunate side of being human: we tend to follow instructions without question."

"Well, that makes me feel a little ashamed. My whole job is based on following orders."

"And you follow these orders without question?"

"Oh no, I ask plenty of questions."

"What types of questions?"

"Well, the average doctor believes a nurse can read his or her mind, and they all believe even more strongly that what is in their minds is absolutely correct, which is, of course, not always correct. So I would say no, I don't follow orders blindly."

"Then I presume that to whatever extent you follow the order to deliver a medication to Mr. Sherman, you will make sure it is the right order for the right patient at the right time. Am I correct?"

"Well, that's my problem. I have no training in this sort of thing. I have no way of knowing if it is right or wrong. I mean, I can't just call up the doctor and say, 'I'm calling to verify the dosage on this prescription. It seems a little low. Are you sure this is enough to kill the man?'"

The Chaplain grinned in response to her attempt at humor, but he did not laugh.

"Ok, I know that was inappropriate. Forgive me. But surely you see my point? When it comes to this question, I'm morally incompetent. It is a no-win situation: either I deliver a medication intended to allow a man to terminate his life; or I refuse to deliver the drug due to my own personal moral ineptitude. Either way, I expect to lie awake tonight feeling guilty about my decision."

Chaplain Moffat's eyes widened in unexpected

pleasure, "I should think that is because you are truly good my dear."

"I do not feel like a good person, Chaplain. I mean, I don't know how I can do good in this case; like you said, authentically good people seem to know just what to say and do in these situations."

"But you admit that you feel guilt. Only a virtuous person would say such a thing; just as only a person with eyes would recognize darkness."

Avalyn replied with an affectionate smile and a humble admission, "You are very kind to say that you see virtue in me, but you should know that I am no saint."

"Do not underestimate your ability to know when something is not right. I suppose philosophers and theologians, those experts in ethics and morality, would recognize the intricate variations on what is good and what is evil similar to the way a master of music could distinguish individual notes in a symphony. But the most amateur musician recognizes when even one instrument in the orchestra is out of tune. So, too, all human beings have an innate sense, first apparent in childhood, the very moment a virtue has been contaminated by vice. It is a universal knowledge passed down from the first moment a man and a woman, who originally knew only good, found it desirable to taste both the good and the evil. The strings have remained a bit out of tune ever since."

Avalyn nodded, "That's it. That is exactly how I feel: out of tune. But I don't think I'm supposed to feel that way about someone else's decision. I take care of a lot of bad people who have done some very bad things. When I learn of the horrible things one of these inmates has done, I may feel bad for the victim, even remorseful. But I don't feel guilty. The criminals can bear that burden alone. So why do I feel guilty in this case? Listen to me. Am I insane? Now I'm feeling guilty about feeling guilty."

"You are quite sane, I can assure you. Very few people are comfortable with the concept of guilt. It sounds too much like sin. But if you perceive something to be wrong, it must be because you also recognize when something is right. I think you would find we all recognize, if only tacitly, that guilt is a protective mechanism. It is to the psyche what pain is to the body. Can you imagine a world where people feel no pain? Pain is protective. It would be a very unhappy world where people were blind or lame from the inability to perceive and remove a damaging shard from the eye or to withdraw a hand or foot from the cause of a burn or puncture of the skin. I should think it equally tragic to think of a world where men and women feel no guilt. I think you must heed to this protective sense, and guard yourself against the temptation to do something that does not yet seem right."

"So why do I feel guilty when very smart people seem to think this is ok?"

"Perhaps you see something they cannot yet see. The modern person, to the extent that he or she is modern, finds value in life, liberty, and conspicuous consumption. Those are the unalienable rights, are they not? Mr. Sherman has lost all three: he lost his liberty due to his crimes; any property he owns is locked away in a warehouse somewhere here in the prison, items he will never see again; and he will soon lose his life. So what happens when a man is alienated from his God-given rights? Are there any sources of dignity left? Death seems like a logical option for people who no longer find meaning or purpose in life. But perhaps you recognize another source of dignity, something more enduring, a virtue that extends beyond the grave."

Avalyn looked at the chaplain and respectfully asked, "So, why do you think this task fell to me? Of all days, why today? And of all people, why me? Surely a thousand other people could satisfy Mr. Sherman's request."

Chaplain Moffat folded his hands in his lap, "I will not presume to speak for God or suggest I know the reasons behind His divine providence. However, I can say that the God who made the earth and everything in it has perfect control of the matter. From Adam forward through every generation, God has chosen the time and exact location of each person's life. This is by design. No one exists by accident. God determines the place and time when each individual is most likely to seek Him, reach out for Him, and find Him, though He is not far from any one of us. If this is true, then I should think that our Mr. Sherman is right here in our infirmary at this very time for a purpose much higher than mere medical care. He is preparing for a meeting with God. You cannot do anything that will hasten, or postpone, that meeting."

The chaplain leaned forward holding his palms together in a prayer-like pose, "But your decision will have a profound impact on you. You, my dear Avalyn, are here in this place and time for a reason as well. I cannot help thinking that something about Mr. Sherman's life and his decision is meant to have some influence on your own search for what is good."

Avalyn looked up at the chaplain; her eyes became moist. His counsel had a depth she was not yet ready to explore fully, but he had given her reason to think about her role in Sherman's death as having more meaning than merely following a medical order.

She slid off the gurney and said, "Thank you for your time and your kindness. I wish I had your confident faith. I'm afraid my conscience is still confused. Mr. Sherman only has to live with his decision long enough to swallow; I will have to live with this the rest of my life."

With that, Avalyn walked to the door. Before walking through, she turned to the chaplain and said, "When you say your prayers, please put in a good word for me, Chaplain."

"My dear Avalyn, you walk in the shadow of death. I pray for you every day."

CHAPTER THIRTEEN

JOSEPH SHERMAN'S CONFESSION

"I did not choose cancer. My life is being taken from me. I am being robbed by mutated cells from my own body. They say I can preserve my dignity by choosing the hour of my death. I can take these pills and claim a freedom to die on my own terms. But this freedom, if you call it freedom at all, is an illusion. My card has been drawn. I am not free. I'm a dead man."

-Joseph E. Sherman
Prison Inmate

Avalyn looked at her watch. The time had come for the afternoon med pass. She walked back to the medication room and began loading the wheeled cart with medications to be distributed to inmates in the infirmary.

She paused before opening the narcotic box. Inside the box before her were three cards containing pills intended to end a man's life. She slid her key into its slot, but then she waited. She did not open the box for several minutes. Voices in her head competed for influence over what she should do next. She felt she could think of a thousand reasons to turn the key and proceed. Giving the medication to Mr. Sherman was legal. It was, in reality, someone else's decision--the doctor bore the ultimate weight of responsibility for the prescription. She was only administering a prescribed medication which was no more or less than what was expected for her scope of practice. But a persistent small voice inside her head perseverated on a single compelling reason to walk away. Mr. Sherman was an evil man. He had killed people in painful unspeakable ways after hours, even days of torture. How could he be given the dignity he craved yet had so viciously denied others?

Still, she felt trapped. Mr. Sherman had her in a checkmate of sorts. He could make a mess of her life and career. He could grieve her refusal to provide him with a prescribed medication and call for a court injunction. He could sue her for deliberate indifference to his pain and suffering. She could lose her license for abandoning a patient.

Avalyn felt an unfamiliar anger welling up within her. Despite working with notoriously irritating individuals, no other inmate had ever found a way to get under her skin. Mr. Sherman was different. He found a way both to irritate and to threaten Avalyn.

As she groped for a solution, she started talking to herself, "I will not let that man ruin my career. Let him face his final judgment; what do I care? I do not have to know why the medication is prescribed. This is between the patient and the doctor. I will just do my job and go home. I refuse to involve myself further."

In anger, with a reddened face and firm, intentional twist of the key, Avalyn opened the cabinet, snatched the three cards of secobarbital, and threw them into the med cart along with the stock medications already prepared for the other inmates.

With slow heavy steps, like an undertaker at a wake, she pushed the medication cart to each cell, beginning with cell number one. Vatel opened the door without saying a word. Avalyn checked the inmate's blood pressure and delivered his afternoon medications. Neither the inmate nor Avalyn spoke.

The scenario was repeated in each room; the infirmary lay quiet in a shroud of ominous stillness. Even the bang of cell doors seemed muffled. Some of the inmates stood at their cell doors watching Avalyn in a reverent silence in anticipation of the finale to this morbid melodrama.

Finally Avalyn pushed the cart to the door of cell number twelve. She looked at the white erase placard just outside the door with the name JOSHEPH SHERMAN written in black ink. Through the window she could see the inmate sitting in a hospital bed. His back was toward the door. Avalyn noticed Mr. Sherman's legs, extended and comfortably crossed. He focused on a book held upright in his hands. She watched as Mr. Sherman licked his finger and flipped the book to the final page. Then, after a moment, Mr. Sherman ran his finger over the closing lines and folded the book closed.

Avalyn whispered to Vatel, "I'm ready for number twelve."

Vatel opened the door. Avalyn reached into the medication cart drawer and removed three bubble pack medication cards, a single anti-nausea pill, and a small drink mix packet. She did not greet Sherman or attempt to check his vital signs. She did not even make eye contact with him, at least not initially. Her hands were shaking, and she knew her voice would do the same. She merely placed the medication packs on a wheeled bedside stand. Next to the medication, she placed a drink mix packet and a paper cup filled with tepid water.

Finally, Avalyn spoke, "Have you been given instructions on how to take your medication?"

"Yes," Sherman replied in a dry sarcastic tone, "It's not that complicated."

Avalyn masked any evidence of emotion. "I am required to remind you that this medication is designated as KOP or keep-on-person. It must be taken as prescribed. It may not be shared. Every capsule should be opened and the powder must be dissolved in liquid prior to ingestion. Any deviation from this prescribed use of the medication will result in confiscation of the remaining medication and loss of KOP privileges. Is this understood?"

Joseph placed his book down beside the medication on the table. He picked up one of the cards and inspected the capsules. Without looking up he asked, "What do you think it means to be free?"

His question took Avalyn off guard. The question itself took her back to her first encounter with Sherman. She was not interested in another lengthy discussion. But his question, the pondering words of a man standing on the edge of death, piqued her curiosity, "Excuse me? I don't take your meaning."

"What does it mean to be truly free?"

"You mean not in prison?"

"I mean free from everything. Can a person truly be unbound? Free from punishment? Free from rules? Free from suffering? Free to make choices and to remain free from consequences? I was not free to decide the day I was born. Would I have been different if I lived a hundred years ago or a hundred years from now? Would I be sitting in a cell if I'd been born in Asia or Africa?"

Sherman looked up to confirm he had the nurse's attention, "And do you think I am really free to choose the time of my death? This terrible choice is forced upon me. I did not choose cancer. My life is being taken from me. I am being robbed by mutated cells from my own body. They say I can preserve my dignity by choosing the hour of my death. I can take these pills and claim a freedom to die on my own terms. But this freedom, if you call it freedom at all, is an illusion. My card has been drawn. I am not free. I'm a dead man."

Then Sherman grinned, his eyes very much alive, "Yet the law has no hold on a dead man; anyone who dies has been freed from consequences. When you walk out that door, my sentence will have been served. I will be free."

Avalyn sensed a manipulative tone in Sherman's contemplation, but he seemed to have insight into his predicament. Her anger at his decision gave way to a new emotion: pity. Without thinking, she reached out a hand and touched Sherman's shoulder, "Are you sure about this, Mr. Sherman?"

Sherman looked at the hand on his shoulder and then at Avalyn. Unless absolutely necessary to perform a medical procedure, nurses do not touch inmates because physical acts of compassion are too easily misinterpreted. Sherman closed his eyes and felt his entire body relax. It was the first time in two decades anyone had given him a kindhearted touch. "You have been very kind, Nurse Robbins. You don't have to be here. We know that. You clearly see things others do not. May I make one final request?"

"Depends. What's your request?"

Sherman pointed toward Vatel, who was standing in silent attention in the cell doorway, "Does he have to be here? I would prefer to ask you something in private."

Avalyn removed her hand from Sherman's shoulder. She crossed her arms. In a curt tone she said, "Officer Vatel stays as long as I do."

"Very well. I'll keep it clean so as not to offend his tender ears."

Avalyn raised an eyebrow. Vatel was unmoved.

Sherman rotated so as to fully face Avalyn. "You may find it hard to believe, though I don't really care what you believe; I was once a decent man. I worked hard with these hands. Even owned my own construction company. Would you believe that I laid the concrete for part of this prison? Ironic, right? But an unfaithful wife and a child killed by an intoxicated driver change a man. Something snapped in me. I sought the comfort of drugs, first pain killers, then straight heroin. I killed a man for pulling a gun on me during a buy. Then came the women. Professional girls who provided companionship for a price. I was judgmental, I admit it. They made me feel dirty, and I felt justified in ridding the world of one or two of them. I've killed several people. Don't look shocked. You knew this or at least suspected it. I don't mind confessing now. A dying man has nothing to hide. I made sure each person's passing was quick and clean. I'm a murderer and an addict, maybe even a thief, I admit it, but I'm not a monster."

Avalyn tapped her foot and rolled her hand as if to speed up time, "What is your request?"

"Be patient with me, I'm getting there. You know the police never caught me. I turned myself in. I just walked into the police station and admitted to my crimes, at least the ones they knew about, all because of what one woman said before she died."

"I'm listening."

"She was a college student who worked at a coffee shop in the evenings. I remember the name embroidered on her shirt: *Lyndsay*. Her pattern was absolutely predictable. The coffee shop closed at eight, and she would walk back to the campus after locking the doors; she was always alone. One night it was raining hard, torrential even, and I was her last customer. I offered her a ride. She was friendly and attractive. I thought she might enjoy the excitement of an experienced man; I invited her to my apartment for drinks and maybe a little more. She refused. She demanded I drop her off right there. She would not even give me her address. She just quietly but firmly kept saying, 'please stop the car.' I became angry, out of my mind really. I drove to an old rock quarry and pulled a gun on her. I pointed the gun at her forehead and told her to unbutton her blouse. She said no. And get this. She did not even look at the gun; she just looked at me with solid brown eyes. Blinking slowly as if confronting a friend she said, 'Mister, you cannot threaten me with going home.'"

Sherman continued, "Her words have haunted me ever since. I pulled the trigger that night; buried the girl under a pile of rocks in an abandoned pit. But I can't get her face or her words out of my head. It was as if she turned the gun on me that night. I felt like a thief who learned he was the one being robbed. She did not fear death. I've never met a person like her before or since.

She did not plead for her life. In fact she pleaded for mine. 'Save yourself; you were not meant for this,' she said. 'Do what you must but know it will not hurt me; it will only destroy you.' I don't mean to say she welcomed death. She just spoke of it as if it were merely a trip somewhere else."

Sherman looked up at Avalyn, "Until now, I did not know what that young saint meant. But now I do. And that leads me to a final request: would you mix the solution and pour it into my mouth? I want to lie still from the first moment to the last. It would be an eternal gift to me. I have caused such suffering in others. I admit it. With these hands I have taken life. My ears still hear their fading screams. It does not seem right that in the end I am given the dignity of a peaceful passing at my own hands. I want to experience what my last victim described; I want to be killed with no fear."

Avalyn listened patiently until that point. She rolled her eyes and let out a long sigh. She felt a growing anger return deep in her chest, "What you are asking is illegal, Mr. Sherman. Either you mix the solution and take the medication on your own, or it will not happen."

Sherman resigned with a grin, "I understand. But permit me at least one more question. I respect your opinion as you are one of the few people who have known me sober. Please tell me, am I making the right choice? Should I take these pills and leave now, you know, on my own terms?"

Avalyn did not give a real answer. Something about the question and the way it was asked fueled the feelings of indignant resentment within her. She crossed her arms and said, "I cannot answer that question for you, Mr. Sherman."

Sherman looked up at Avalyn. He slid forward with his hand placed firmly on the edge of the bed as if ready to stand, "It's my choice. I accept that. I'm not asking anyone to make the choice for me. I'm just asking for your opinion. Why is it so hard for people to answer a simple question? I know it is my choice. But is it the right choice?"

Avalyn felt inhibition give way to unrestrained candid honesty. She pivoted into a defensive stance and stood ready to shuffle back through the cell door at any sign of aggression. "All I can say is that it sounds like not everyone of your acquaintance has had that choice."

Sherman's eyes became suddenly red with anger. He raised a violent fist in the air and screamed, "Get this judgmental whore out of my room."

CHAPTER FOURTEEN

CHANGE OF HEART

"Ever see a man die from cancer? He would have been in the ICU for weeks, fed with a PEG tube, surrounded by monitors and lines. And all for what? Sherman was a useless eater, a life unworthy of life. Don't waste one minute grieving for that man."

- Gloria Wirth, RN
Nursing Supervisor

Avalyn backed out of the cell. Sherman was still yelling obscenities muffled by the glass window as she pushed the medication cart back to the nurses' desk in slow, solemn silence, bent forward as in the final steps of a hard journey. Then with sluggish fingers she typed out final progress notes for the record.

Vatel shut Joseph Sherman's cell door with emphatic force and returned to his station. On the monitor he could see Sherman in his cell. After several minutes of cursing at the window, he stopped yelling and sat down on his bedside. At one point he picked up a card of capsules. Perhaps he was still contemplating his options. *What a wretched man*, thought Vatel. *What kind of person chooses to die alone in a prison?*

Vatel watched the inmate for a moment. Then per orders from the superintendent he reached forward and flipped a small switch on the control panel; the monitor in cell number twelve went black.

For the next few minutes Avalyn and Vatel completed their respective documentation in an unfamiliar silence. They each respected the other's need to process the role they had been asked to play in the final day of a man's life.

Finally Avalyn pushed the keyboard to the back of her desk and placed her head in the palm of both hands. Her eyes and nose swelled with moisture. Avalyn knew she would have to leave. Displays of emotion were discouraged in the presence of inmates. So she wiped her nose with a tissue and stood to walk toward the exit, "Officer Vatel, I'll be off the floor for a while. Radio if I'm needed."

Vatel acknowledged her departure with a brief glance. He poured himself a cup of coffee from an insulated drink container and leaned back to observe the infirmary in subdued contemplation.

Avalyn walked out of the infirmary and made her way to the back of the prison where a door led into a private open-air concrete walled courtyard lined with poorly trimmed shrubs and randomly placed rusty tables. A sign outside the exit door read EMPLOYEES ONLY. Avalyn found a place to sit atop one of the tables. She looked up at the grey sky and wept, softly at first, then bitterly. *What have I done?* she thought. At times she cried so hard that she had trouble breathing, her chest tight from the emotional angina of a heart broken, crushed by the thought of having done something evil.

After several minutes, Avalyn heard the door behind her squeak. She wiped each eye with the palm of her hand and sat up erect to feign composure. She did not look back but became alert to the sound of footsteps approaching her from behind. For about a minute, Avalyn felt the eyes of someone watching.

Finally a woman with a coarse voice said, "Need a smoke?"

Avalyn turned to see her supervisor, Gloria Wirth

holding out a cigarette.

"No, thank you. I haven't smoked since college," said Avalyn.

"Well you're looking rough today. Mind if I have one for you?"

Gloria sat down next to Avalyn. She smoothly lit a cigarette and exhaled a stream of smoke, "I've been working here over thirty years. And there is one thing I've learned: there's nothing behind these walls worth crying over. What's got under your skin?"

Avalyn wiped away a straggling tear, "I feel like I've made a terrible mistake."

Gloria flicked ash from the tip of her cigarette, "Are you upset about Sherman's case?"

Avalyn nodded. Her mind raced through the events of the day, "I have been under a black cloud all day. You know I was late for work. We had a suicide attempt this morning. And when the doctor sprung Sherman's case on me, I didn't know what to do." Avalyn's eyes began to well up again, "Gloria, I gave him the pills that will end his life. I did not want to do it. But the order fell to me. You said I had no choice. I expect any minute to be called back to medical. Mr. Sherman will be lying there stiff and breathless without a pulse. I was the last one to see him alive and I'll be the first one to see him dead, dead from pills that I handed him."

"Good riddance, I say. Doctor Brant did us all a favor. Ever see a man die from cancer? He would have been in the ICU for weeks, fed with a PEG tube, surrounded by monitors and lines. And all for what? Sherman was a useless eater, a life unworthy of life. Don't waste one minute grieving for that man."

"It's not him I am concerned about. He asked me to give him the medication. I mean he asked me actually to pour it into his mouth. I refused. I reasoned it was his choice. I'm a nurse, a healer. I'm not a killer. But I left the pills at his bedside. What's the difference? It's not grief I feel; it is guilt."

Gloria tossed her cigarette butt into the cigarette receptacle, "See, you've got a conscience. That's something ol' Mr. Sherman never had. Never shed one tear over the suffering he caused. Now he's got you crying like a baby. But what gives you the right to carry a burden of guilt that belongs to him? Were you there when he killed those people? Tell me. Did you stand there watching? Did you sell him the gun? Did you teach him how to kill? Were you his accomplice? See, you've got me speaking like a crazy woman. You are not guilty; he is. He is a selfish man who allowed other human beings to suffer and die because it felt right for him. Now he's psychologically ravaged you."

Something in those final words resonated with Avalyn. Though coarse and offensive, Gloria's editorial somehow unlocked a fuller understanding of what to that point had only been an ethereal sentiment that dissipated at any attempt to grasp words to describe her emotion. Avalyn turned and looked directly at Gloria. Her voice continued to crack with emotion as her heart pounded anticipation of finally being able verbally to identify the source of her pain, "That's it. That's why this is all wrong.

He's a killer. I am a healer. I don't want to become like him. I refuse. But Gloria, today I crossed a line. I am a nurse. I am committed to provide care for a man until his last breath, but today I went too far. I helped a man take his last breath. I feel like I've done something terrible, something I will never be able to take back."

Avalyn again wept. She placed both hands over her eyes and bent forward sobbing under a burden of guilt.

Gloria extended her arm around Avalyn in a display of silent compassion. She pulled Avalyn close and for several minutes allowed Avalyn to cry in her arms.

Then, as her tears slowed, Avalyn pulled away. She felt a mix of appreciation and embarrassment. She was thankful for Gloria's kindness but embarrassed by her own emotional breakdown in front of her supervisor. She wiped the tears from her face and stood up. She took a deep breath to regain her composure and said, "Thank you, Gloria. I need to go. But thank you."

Avalyn sluggishly walked back toward the infirmary with her head held low. She felt the weight of shame, torn about how to bear this strange burden. She knew she should return to her post, but she did not know if she was ready for what awaited her there. Then another thought struck her; Vatel was still there. What terrible burden was he bearing? She was suddenly overcome by a growing sense of obligation born not from a professional commitment to attend to her duties, but from a personal feeling of remorse; it had been unfair to leave Vatel in the infirmary alone. She imagined him faithfully standing watch over Sherman's final breaths. Was he prepared for such a task? Surely he needed her support as much as she needed his. They were a strange pair, a nurse and an officer, assigned to stand vigil over another human's personal act of self-destruction. Neither of them was trained to serve in this capacity. They needed each other. It was solely this thought of supporting Vatel, her friend who found countless ways to give her courage, which motivated her to return to the infirmary.

But before she made it to the infirmary door, she abruptly turned and headed down a side hallway. There was someone else she needed to speak to first. Only one person really knew how to make things clear for her.

She quickly made her way down a back corridor and paused in front of the nurses' lounge. She did not enter right away. She felt uneasy about having to explain her swollen, tearstained eyes to any colleague who happened to be taking a break, so she opened the door slowly and peered inside as if looking to see if the room were clear. The lounge was empty.

Avalyn let out a relieved sigh and took a seat on the couch. After collecting her thoughts she picked up the telephone and dialed the number for home. Her foot tapped restlessly on the floor. *I need you*, she thought. *Please be home.*

The phone rang several times. Avalyn felt her heart sink a little further in her chest with each successive ring. *Where are you?* Then she heard her own voice in a message over the phone, "You have reached the Robbins' residence. Please leave a message...beep."

Avalyn hung up and then dialed her husband's cell

phone. There was no ring. The line went immediately to voice mail. Avalyn paused. She did not want to alarm her husband, but she needed him. She needed to hear his voice. She sought his protection. But she struggled with how to word a message. *Why doesn't he answer?* She cleared her throat and tried to mask her trembling voice, "Hi, Babe. Um, I need to talk to you. When you get the message, please give me a call here at work...call the lounge."

She left the number of the nurses' lounge and hung up. She felt very alone. She did not want to return to the infirmary, though that was her post, and Vatel would need her medical support. But she could not summon the courage to return; not without talking with her husband. *Has Sherman already taken the pills? What if he has already passed? Surely Vatel would radio if something happened.*

Finally she resigned herself to the thought that the inevitable conclusion was beyond her control. She stood and slowly walked toward the door. As she reached for the door handle, the phone behind her rang. Avalyn rushed back to the phone and anxiously grabbed the receiver. She instinctively answered as if taking a professional call, "Department of Corrections, this is Nurse Robbins."

Officer Robbins laughed on the other line, "Hi Ave, sorry I missed your call. This little girl of ours just blew out a diaper. What's going on?"

Avalyn suddenly froze at the sound of her husband's voice. She was unable to move or to answer. The sound of home and all that was dear to her hit her like a shockwave and knocked the wind out of her. She felt as if she could not breathe. She finally managed to take a few short breaths and said, "Babe, I need your help. I feel like I've made a terrible mistake."

"What's wrong, Ave? You sound shook up."

"It's awful, Babe. I feel awful."

"Tell me what's going on. You need me to come in?"

"No, I'll be fine. I just needed to hear your voice."

"Tell me what happened, Ave. Are you hurt?"

"No, I'm ok. It's just Sherman. Did you hear he's supposed to die today?"

"Hard to miss. It's all over the news. But don't let him get to you. Sherman's just being a jerk. Did you get stuck with him today?"

"Yes, I'm covering the infirmary. Brant came by this morning and wrote the final script for Sherman's meds. This afternoon they delivered the pills to end his life."

"Oh, Ave, what happened?"

Avalyn was overcome with emotion and started sobbing. She held her hand over the phone to hide the sound until she could speak, "I gave him the pills. I didn't want to. I told them I wasn't comfortable. But it's my job. Brant left after rounds. And you know Sherman. He's a creep. He insisted on taking them today. I get the idea people are happy to see him go. But he's dying, alone. I don't want to go back in there and find him dead from something I gave him. But that's what's going to happen."

"Ave, he's not worth it. You don't owe that man anything. Don't let him do this to you. Can you go take the pills back? Just tell them you can't be a part of this. Let someone else take over."

"I can't do that, Babe. I already gave him the medication. If I take it back now, it will cause a firestorm. They could report me to the board for negligence or abandonment. He could sue us personally. I could lose my license. We've got the kids and the house. We barely get by as it is. We can't afford for me to get fired."

"Ave, listen to me. You do not have to do this. Don't let them pressure you. I love you. Your kids love you. Work is just what you do; it's not who you are. I'll work overtime. If they choose to threaten you, that's on them. You can go anywhere. They will never find another nurse like you. You do the right thing, Ave, that's what you do. That's who you are. Me and the cubs here are behind you one hundred percent."

Avalyn smiled and quietly laughed at the thought of being home. She sensed the welcome return of courage, "Thank you, Babe. That is just what I needed to hear. I can't wait to see you."

"We can't wait to see you too."

Just then a shift whistle blew with a high-pitched scream like an old factory whistle to indicate it was two in the afternoon, the beginning of a mid-shift when about a third of the officers leave for the late afternoon.

Avalyn leapt to her feet. She wiped her eyes, "That sounds like a sign to me. I've got to return to the infirmary. See you in a few hours." She hung up and exited the nurses' lounge.

CHAPTER FIFTEEN

FREEDOM

"He seems to be in a coma. Do we know what happened?"

- Will Farrow
Municipal Paramedic

As Avalyn headed down the corridor toward the infirmary, she was met by a group of officers making their way toward the sally port exit. They moved down the hallway in an undulating mass, a jovial, loud-mouthed wave of blue, joking as they headed home after a long shift. For them, the workday was over.

The officers respectfully parted as Avalyn walked past, her countenance focused and serious by contrast. She did not look directly at any of the officers, an oversight she would later regret. Had she been alert, she might have noticed the one who bumped her shoulder as he passed.

Avalyn entered the infirmary. The area felt empty. Vatel's seat was unoccupied; a solitary stream of steam still rose from a cup of coffee on his desk. Perhaps he was counting inmates. She called out, "Officer Vatel. I need to access to cell twelve."

The words were barely out of her mouth when she turned the corner to see the door to cell twelve already open. Avalyn's eyes widened.

She sensed danger and instinctively looked behind her. The scene was chilling. Inmates dressed in orange garb stood behind each cell window watching her in somber silence. Every inmate looked right at her, each one with a tight-jawed, judgmental stare. *Why are they glaring at me? What is going on? Did Vatel leave?*

Avalyn felt her heart's pounding. With a trembling hand, she reached for the radio at her hip and took cautious steps toward cell twelve.

Through the open door, she could see the shape of a body slumped over the bed under a thin blanket. Avalyn felt suddenly nauseous. "I'm too late," Avalyn whispered under her breath. As she approached the cell, she noticed a wadded set of orange prison clothes tossed haphazardly on the floor just inside the cell door. She thought it strange that Mr. Sherman had removed his clothes. She imagined that he must have become delirious under the influence of the medication before he fell unconscious.

She keyed the radio, "Control, this is med one, can you locate officer Vatel and page the medical response team to the infirmary."

"We show Officer Vatel just clocked out," control responded. "I will alert the medical team now."

This can't be, thought Avalyn. *Vatel worked the full day shift. He was not scheduled to clock out for hours.*

Avalyn ran into the cell. She ripped the blanket off the body before her and with both hands, she rolled the man onto his back. As the man's face pivoted into view Avalyn yelled, "Vatel!"

It was Vatel, not Sherman, who lay on the bed in front of her. Avalyn reached for Vatel's neck to check for a pulse while with the other hand she struggled to key her radio, "Officer down in the infirmary. Need EMS and officer back up immediately!"

Avalyn felt strong carotid pulsations, "Stay with me, Vatel," she said. She bent forward to place her cheek just over Vatel's mouth. She felt Vatel's sour, warm breath rush out against her skin. Just then Vatel awoke briefly and looked at Avalyn with a glassy, somnolent stare and then fell listless again. Reassured that he was at least still alive, though unresponsive, she situated Vatel's head and body in a position to protect his airway.

Avalyn's attention returned to securing the scene, "Control this is med one. Advise lock down. We are missing an inmate."

"Initiating lock down. Can you identify the inmate?" asked control.

Avalyn keyed her microphone, "His name is Joseph Sherman."

Three other officers arrived on the scene, followed shortly by another nurse and two paramedics. The paramedics took charge of the medical scene. Working in concert with each other, they performed a series of choreographed medical procedures. They placed Vatel on a monitor, started an intravenous line, and provided him with low-dose oxygen. The older of the medics, a muscular man with a grey crew cut who wore a blue t-shirt and fireman gear from the waist down turned to speak with Avalyn, "He seems to be in a coma. Do we know what happened?"

Avalyn watched the paramedics perform the rapid assessment on Officer Vatel. She felt her legs going limp, perhaps in an early stage of emotional shock. Her mind began to wander. Every thought seemed to center on getting home safely to see her little ones and her husband. The paramedic's question instantly brought her attention back to the emergency at hand. She stumbled over the first few words, but once mentally primed, she was able to brief the paramedics with professional efficiency on what little she knew. Suddenly the thought struck her and she said, "The pills. Where are the pills? This man may have been poisoned. The inmate in this room had a lethal dose of a sedative."

That was all the paramedics needed to hear. The paramedics transferred Vatel's sleeping, flaccid body to a rolling gurney and rushed him out of the infirmary and out of the prison to a waiting ambulance outside.

The officers performed a count of the inmates in the infirmary. All inmates were accounted for except one: Joseph Sherman.

Avalyn walked back to the nurses' desk. She overheard one of the officers speaking on the phone, "Yes, Superintendent, that is correct. We believe the inmate may have escaped to another part of the facility. We are on lock-down at this time."

Another officer stood at the security post reviewing the monitors. At one point he called out to the others, "Hey, here's your answer. Come look."

Avalyn stood behind the officers as they reviewed the video footage. One of the officers pointed to various areas on the screen and narrated the scene as the others looked on, "The video in cell twelve is dark. We are unable to see what is occurring in there. The monitor had been turned off. But watch closely what happens when

Officer Vatel is approached by the custodial inmate. See there. First the inmate who is holding a broom walks up to Officer Vatel and points in the opposite direction toward cell number seven. Officer Vatel stands and walks to cell number seven. He appears to be listening to a question from the inmate through the cell window. But watch closely at the bottom of the screen. Something slides out of cell twelve. There. See it? Sherman was fishing. The disc is caught by the custodial inmate's broom. He reaches down and picks something up. It is something small. Then he leans over the desk and appears to shake whatever it is into Officer Vatel's cup here on the table. Next he turns and tosses an object into the garbage can. Thirty seconds later Officer Vatel returns to his desk and takes a sip of his coffee."

The lieutenant looked at one of his officers, "Get me the name of that worker. Who was on the schedule? Is he from Echo?"

Avalyn looked at the time stamp on the video. It read 13:49:17, and she remembered the coded message seen in segregation. Now it made sense to her. The sweeper at two in the afternoon. This was a coordinated plan. Avalyn rushed to the garbage can. She threw off the lid and sifted through the debris. There, near the top was the drug, or at least the empty capsules. She turned to the officers and said, "Here. Look, three empty capsules. Officer Vatel was poisoned."

The officer reviewed the remainder of the footage which showed Officer Vatel turning his head toward cell twelve as if he had been called over. He stood up quickly and walked to cell twelve, opening the door with his key. Once he entered the cell, nothing could be seen because the individual cell monitor had been shut off. Five minutes later, Vatel appeared to exit the cell, his cap pulled low over his face.

One officer pointed at the screen, "Wait. Replay the moment the officer walks out the door. Something is not right. He is carrying keys alright. But he is not wearing his service belt. No cuffs. No radio. Why would he remove these?"

"That's not officer Vatel. His pants are too short. And look at the way the other inmates seem to be standing and clapping at their cell windows. That is Sherman. He disguised himself in the officer's uniform."

As if in a collective moment of realization the truth hit them simultaneously. One officer articulated the conclusion at which they all had arrived, "Sherman attempted to escape at shift change."

"Surely not. He would have to pass through security."

Avalyn said, "When I called control, they reported that Officer Vatel left the building at shift change."

Lieutenant Burke radioed master control, "Control, Burke, please verify status of Officer Vatel on the infirmary post."

"Standby," was the initial reply followed fifteen seconds later by the response, "Lieutenant, Control, we show Officer Vatel clocked out at fourteen o 'five."

"Are you sure it was Officer Vatel?"

"My men say he passed through the port with around twenty others at shift change. He traded his identification badge and facility keys in for his personal keys. We can review the footage."

Lieutenant Burke turned to one of his officers, "Get me the superintendent on the phone."

Just then another officer walked out of cell twelve holding a wide black leather belt. A set of handcuffs and a radio hung from the clips on the belt. The officer held up the service belt, "This was under the mattress, sir. The room is otherwise clear. Only personal items remain. Except we also found this note tucked under the bed frame."

The Lieutenant took the piece of paper and read aloud the penciled message, "PILL PASS TODAY BEFORE TWO."

Avalyn suddenly remembered Sherman's request to Vatel. Her eyes opened wide as when suddenly seeing the solution to a difficult puzzle. So that's why he requested that his room be cleaned. The inmate must have known to look for the note and follow the instructions to be sweeping the infirmary at just the right time.

Then the message itself caught her full attention. Pill pass at two? She grabbed the officer's arm, "What about medication? The inmate was issued a large number of pills."

"Negative, ma'am. There are no pills in the room. We will have maintenance check the plumbing filters to see if anything has been discarded in the drain or toilet."

An officer called to the Lieutenant with his palm held over the telephone, "Superintendent Washington is on line one."

Lieutenant Burke reached for the phone. He ran a hand over the top of his head as he spoke, "Sir, we have an unfortunate situation. We believe Inmate Sherman has escaped the facility. He appears to have absconded while disguised as an officer. He is assumed to have a lethal dose of a pharmaceutical agent still in his possession. We believe he is either on foot or traveling in a stolen vehicle. We know he obtained the personal keys, including car keys, which belong to Officer Frantz Vatel. The police department and troopers need to be alerted. Do you have further orders sir?"

The Lieutenant listened and acknowledged understanding. At one point he pulled out his notepad and began scribbling an itemized list. Then he looked up toward Avalyn, "Yes sir, I will ask her."

Lieutenant Burke was a man accustomed to giving orders; he was not well versed in diplomatically asking others for help, especially if outside his sphere of command. His profession depended on decisive action, not surveys of personal preference, "Nurse Robbins, the superintendent requests that you accompany me as the designated medical escort should the inmate be apprehended and need transport to a hospital or back to the prison."

Avalyn felt like the request came across more as a directive than an appeal. She raised an eyebrow as a reminder that medical personnel were not under the command of the prison's security staff.

The lieutenant saw her response and bowed his head slightly in a nod of respect, "Would you kindly accept

Superintendent Washington's request?"

Avalyn looked back at the lieutenant. She appreciated the lieutenant's genuine attempt to overcome his reluctance in asking for help; she responded with a grin, and then she reached under the desk, pulling out the emergency response bag. With the bag strap over a shoulder, she said, "We are not waiting on me."

CHAPTER SIXTEEN

SLEIGHT OF HAND

"If this day should end well, I will be transporting our prisoner back to a maximum security segregated cell."

- Lieutenant John Burke
Department of Corrections

Avalyn exited the prison atrium with Lieutenant Burke. The lieutenant had donned a bulletproof vest and carried a visible service weapon on his belt. Avalyn instinctively lowered her head and followed the lieutenant. The pressing crowd of reporters and demonstrators separated reluctantly, allowing the pair to pass.

Once clear of the crowd, Burke started walking at a rapid, anxious pace. He looked over his shoulder at Avalyn as he pointed toward the back parking lot, "We will take one of the transport vans."

Burke unlocked one of the vans, a black, windowless passenger van labeled Department of Corrections with an added warning for would-be curious onlookers: Do Not Approach. The lieutenant jumped into the driver's seat and started the engine.

Avalyn tossed her equipment into the back of the van and climbed into the passenger seat. Her heart pounded with anticipation. She buckled in, pulling the seatbelt with vigor, tight across her lap. "Which way did he go?" she asked.

"First we wait, and we listen," answered Burke. The lieutenant reached forward and twisted a knob of the dispatch radio on the dashboard.

The radio squeaked with chatter as position reports

volleyed among correction officers, police officers, and state troopers positioned throughout the city. Avalyn and Burke sat listening for several minutes.

During a pause in the radio reports, Avalyn commented on the lieutenant's attire, "I don't recall ever seeing you with a weapon, Lieutenant."

"Weapons are issued to transport officers. Those of us who move prisoners receive special training in the use of firearms and restraint techniques. My attire is a vote for a hopeful outcome. If this day should end well, I will be transporting our prisoner back to a maximum security segregated cell."

The dispatcher broke in, "Be advised: suspect is likely dressed as a law enforcement officer. Video from the corrections department shows the inmate departed the prison employee parking lot in a white pickup truck."

Avalyn looked at the lieutenant, "He must have taken Vatel's old truck. Where would he be headed?"

"I would think he needs to find a nearby location to lay low."

"There's the homeless shelter about a mile from the prison. He could see it from the prison. Do you think he would stay that close?"

"Not a bad thought. Many of the people at that establishment have been through our doors, some of them as regulars. Even if Sherman himself is not there, I would not be surprised if our best informants were to be found among the clientele at the shelter."

Lieutenant Burke and Avalyn drove to the shelter, a converted warehouse owned by the city, which served as a housing facility and feeding station for the city's less fortunate souls.

Many clients at the shelter were also frequent guests at the prison. For some, it was a way of life, a cycle between the freedom of summers at the shelter, which included a daily bowl of soup and a safe place to roll out a mattress, and survival through the winters by strategically orchestrating a stay in prison during the long, cold months in order to maintain access to high-calorie meals and a warm place to sleep, all of which is statutorily mandated at the State's expense. Avalyn recalled hearing an inmate quip, "We know which crimes will earn us three hots and a cot."

The lieutenant approached a series of people gathered on the shelter's front porch. It was clear that many of the residents knew the lieutenant. He even called some of them by name. But it was equally clear that they were not interested in talking with him, their eyes held low while backing away as if trying to escape slowly without notice.

They knew something. The typically curious masses, concerned for their own safety or wellbeing, would be expected to surround an officer and ask questions to learn any news of a locally escaped prisoner. The shelter residents, on the other hand, quietly withdrew from the lieutenant. Perhaps it was his intimidating gear or merely the fact that he was a known authority at the prison. Avalyn suspected they had information, if not a full knowledge of Sherman's location.

Avalyn saw the people backing away from the lieutenant. She felt a surge of emotional urgency, and without thinking, yelled from the van, "Please friends. Mr. Joseph Sherman is a very sick man. We need your help. He needs your help. Please tell the lieutenant what you know. You may be able to save the man's life."

Just then the sound of a revving engine and the accelerating screech of tires echoed from the other side of the shelter. A white truck shot out of an alley into the street and sped off toward the highway.

Lieutenant Burke saw the departing vehicle. He stood up to get a clear view. Then he reached for a handset on his shoulder and keyed the microphone, "Dispatch, Burke. The suspect's vehicle has just been identified departing the downtown shelter with two, I repeat, two occupants. Gender of the passenger is unknown. They appear to be headed toward the highway."

The lieutenant ran back to the van. He bounded into the driver's seat and threw the transmission into drive while simultaneously pressing the gas. As the van sped out of the parking area, Burke yelled over the high-pitched engine, "Sherman's got a passenger. Keep your eyes on that truck."

The sudden acceleration threw Avalyn back in her seat. She felt a surge of panic. Her mind filled rapidly with unarticulated questions. *What if Sherman's intent is to kill someone else? What if he kills himself in public? Maybe he is heading somewhere private to die?* Her legs bounced with a nervous energy. She could see the truck pulling away. The unwelcome thought of losing Sherman was too much to contain; she looked at the lieutenant and issued what sounded like an order, "Please drive faster, Lieutenant!"

Lieutenant Burke made an accelerating skid from the parking lot. His attention remained focused on the road as he answered Avalyn, "This is a transport van, not a pursuit vehicle. There's no telling what Vatel's pile of junk can do. Just keep an eye on him."

Avalyn looked intently ahead as the getaway truck crested a small hill over which she could not see. She sat up erect to peer over the rise. Then suddenly a city bus pulled out in front of the van spewing a rising trail of faint grey exhaust. For a matter of seconds, she lost sight of the white truck.

Burke wove around the bus in an almost constant state of acceleration.

Avalyn looked up to see the light ahead turn yellow, then red, and then cross traffic filled the intersection, "Watch out!"

Burke saw the traffic before them and slammed hard on the brakes. The van came to a stop a few feet into the intersection. Several cars swerved around the front of the van, horns blaring, to avoid a collision. Burke slammed his hands on the wheel. "How could we be so close?"

Avalyn pointed ahead. Down the other side of the hill she could see the truck about half a mile away turning onto the main highway. She pointed and exclaimed, "There he goes. Go. Go. Go."

Burke lifted his hand toward the traffic light, "We're stuck. We have no lights. We have no siren. Nobody pulls over for a Department of Corrections van. He's gone. Curse this van. And curse Sherman. We were so close."

The lieutenant keyed his microphone, "Dispatch,

Burke. Please advise the police department and troopers that the suspect is northbound on Highway One just north of the prison complex."

Burke clipped the microphone back onto the dash radio. He turned to Avalyn and said, "He will be out of the city limits in no time. He is in the troopers' jurisdiction now. It's out of our hands."

Avalyn's voice became desperate, "Can't we at least follow him?"

"We are a liability at this point. Let's just head that direction and see what happens. The troopers have a helicopter overhead. Once they intercept Sherman and the truck, it will be a short pursuit."

Avalyn sat in uncomfortable silence.

After several minutes had passed the dispatch radio broke the quiet, "All departments, be advised that Air Command has confirmed the suspect's vehicle is traveling northbound out of town on Highway One approximately five miles north of the city center."

A trooper's voice acknowledged the message, "Copy that, dispatch. We are en route to intercept suspect."

Avalyn and Lieutenant Burke drove slowly northward, listening to the pursuit unfold over the dispatch radio. Avalyn closed her eyes. She could hear sirens in the background as troopers radioed in position reports. In her mind she could piece together the events based only on verbally broadcast snapshots. As she listened, she felt the adrenaline rush of the chase as if she were there in a pursuit vehicle; her heart started pounding, and sweat formed on her forehead.

"We have two pursuit cars directly behind the suspect now. We are full lights and sirens. Suspect is not yielding."

"Roger that. Maintain visual contact, keeping safe distance and speed."

"Troopers are establishing road blocks at major exits."

"Suspect vehicle is swerving erratically. There is a high probability the driver is intoxicated."

"Request permission to execute a PIT."

Avalyn looked at Burke, "What's a PIT?"

"It means Precision Immobilization Technique. It's where the pursuit vehicle executes a controlled impact to the rear of the getaway vehicle to cause a skidding stop."

"I'm not so sure Vatel will appreciate hearing that his truck was involved in a high speed crash."

Another trooper broke over the radio, "Negative. PIT is not authorized. Maintain visual contact at reduced speeds."

Suddenly a trooper broke in with pressured speech, "Suspect has taken the State Park exit. Has that exit been secured?"

"Negative. Park officials have been notified to clear public areas, but the road has not been blocked. Maintain visual contact."

"That may be difficult. The park roads are impossibly serpiginous."

"Quit using words we don't know."

"Roger that," answered the trooper. Then speaking in a juvenile voice as if talking to a child in grade school, he said, "Listen up, students, these roads are thin and very curvy. I think it will be hard to keep up with the bad man in the fast truck."

"Ok, boys, cut the chatter. Let's keep this professional."

"Roger. Does anyone have a map of this park? I want a blockade of all exit routes."

"Please confirm suspects are still in sight."

"Affirmative. They are exiting the forest on the back side of the park."

"Air Command has suspect in sight. The truck is now off the road. He is traveling westbound across the open field toward the lake. His progress has slowed."

"Unit four has suspect in sight. I am crossing the field in pursuit, but my speed is impeded by the mud and tall grass."

"Unit two, expect to turn right onto Shoreline Road. This will place you in line with the suspect's current direction."

"Unit two. Acknowledged. Taking Shoreline Road now."

"Unit three is on the south end of the field. There is a hill that blocks my view of the lake, but I see mud flying in that direction."

"Unit three. Air command confirms your location. Continue your current course to intercept suspect."

"Unit four is closing in on suspect. This guy seems confused. He is not keeping a straight path."

"Unit two is in position on Shoreline Road. Suspect is in sight. He is traveling toward me. He has no options without going into the lake."

A voice broke in with the sound of helicopter blades beating in the background, "All units, the suspect appears to have come to a stop."

"The truck is stuck. He's spinning wheels in the mud. I'm moving in behind him."

"Approaching flank on driver's side at a hundred yards."

"I'll hold his attention from the front. Cover my back; this guy may be armed."

The volume of asynchronous sirens increased in the background as the sound of each car approached the other from opposite sides of the suspect's truck, "All units, close in tight."

"He's throwing mud. The truck is stuck. He's not going anywhere.

"Unit four is moving to apprehend. Video monitor is active."

"Stay alert. Suspect has opened driver's side door."

"Stay in your car! I repeat stay in your car! Place your hands on the wheel and do not move!"

"Keep your weapons ready. Surround and apprehend. Stay alert."

One of the troopers shouted orders which could be heard over the radio, "Step from the vehicle. Keep your hands visible."

"Air Command confirms two persons exiting the vehicle."

"Roger that, Air Command. Report when suspects are in custody."

A trooper's voice came over the radio. The escalating anxiety in previous communications had faded to an almost hushed tone, "Uh, central command, this is Trooper Barnes. I have the suspects in custody, but I don't think this is your man."

"Can you explain?"

The trooper answered over competing sirens heard blaring in the background, "We have two inebriates in custody. Neither fits the description of the suspect."

"Do they have information regarding the suspect?"

"Possibly. They say a uniformed officer at the shelter gave them twenty dollars each to deliver the truck to his mother's house north of town."

"Did they disclose an address?"

"Negative. They're drunk. The driver says they forgot where they were going so they headed for the lake for a little R and R, and I don't mean rest and relaxation. I questioned them about running from us. He claims they thought we were an escort."

Avalyn started to shift in her seat. She looked at Lieutenant Burke, "Could one of them be Sherman?"

The Lieutenant keyed the radio microphone, "Central command, this is Lieutenant Burke with the Department of Corrections. Can you identify either of the people you have in custody? Could either one of them be Joseph Sherman?"

"Neither occupant has identification. The passenger is female and cannot be your man. Can you give us a visual description of Mr. Sherman?"

"He is male less than six feet tall with a clean shaven

scalp and tattooed chest."

The trooper interrupted before Lieutenant Burke could finish, "Negative. The driver has a full head of hair and beard; unless we're dealing with a man who possesses werewolf qualities, I'd say this is not your escapee."

Avalyn listened to the report. Information was coming in stilted radio communications, but reality poured in all at once. She looked at Lieutenant Burke, "Sherman is somewhere else."

Lieutenant Burke had already given action to this very thought. He reversed course by making a bouncing turn within the grass-covered median. He pushed the gas pedal to the floorboard, timing his merge with speeding traffic in the southbound lane.

As the Department of Corrections van sped south, Avalyn asked, "So where are we heading?"

"Back to the shelter; maybe Sherman ditched the truck and is still hiding."

CHAPTER SEVENTEEN

SHERMAN'S LAST STAND

"The entire world was focused on his death. And he gave them what they wanted: a controversy, a good show. Then having acted out the final scene, he just slipped off the stage."

- Avalyn Robbins, RN
Prison Nurse

Upon arriving at the shelter, Lieutenant Burke leapt from the van and ran toward the front doors of the shelter, his right hand maintaining a firm grasp of his sidearm as he moved quickly in a guarded, almost shuffling gait, his eyes scanning the crowd amassed around the shelter's entrance.

Without a second thought, Avalyn jumped from the van. She had no weapon or plan, only her wits and her desire to find Sherman alive. She intently looked into the face of the individuals standing around the shelter. It was obvious that she was looking for one specific person.

Burke pushed a path through the people on the porch and entered a large crowded room. Several hundred people stood around the room in small groups or reclined on mats placed in parallel rows around the perimeter.

Through the open double-door entrance, Avalyn watched Burke survey the main hall and proceed toward a cafeteria-style section in the back of the shelter where disheveled men and woman sat in aluminum chairs sharing bowls of soup and bread at rickety tables.

Near the entrance, Avalyn came across an elderly woman with kind eyes and a weather-worn face, her cheeks wrinkled into a near-permanent smile. Avalyn squatted to speak with her, "Excuse me, ma'am, I work at the prison over across the way. I'm looking for an officer who may have been here earlier. He is about my height and was wearing a blue uniform. Have you seen anyone like that?"

The elderly woman shook her head, refusing to speak.

Unexpectedly, Avalyn felt a firm hand on her shoulder. She looked up to see the lieutenant standing over her. He pointed toward the van and said, "Quick, follow me."

The lieutenant jogged back to the department van. Avalyn ran after him.

Once in the van, the lieutenant wasted no time; he turned the key and revved the engine. With tires screeching, the van flew out of the shelter parking area, accelerating in the direction of the highway.

Avalyn grasped a handle on the dash in front of her and reflexively pressed her feet on the floor board as if to slow things down. She yelled, "What's going on? Where are we going?"

"They've located Sherman," Lieutenant Burke said while reaching to turn on the communication radio. The dispatcher broadcast an announcement, "Suspect is thought to be on Metro bus number fifty-seven. The bus is now southbound on the highway toward the city center."

The lieutenant sped around slower moving vehicles and then made an abrupt right merge cutting between two cars, barely making it onto the highway ramp. Avalyn felt the van lean sharply to one side as they veered onto the highway. She held her breath and instinctively leaned in the opposite direction as if she alone could prevent the van from flipping in the accelerated turn.

The lieutenant, in lieu of having lights and a siren, blinked his headlights and blew the van's horn as he sped past cars on the highway.

Avalyn could see the city skyline slowly coming into view on the horizon with office buildings backlit by the softer light of late afternoon.

The lieutenant gripped the wheel and looked at Avalyn, "So why do you think he ran? You knew Sherman; did you see this coming?"

"Of course not; Sherman talked a lot about being free again, but they all talk that way."

"But this guy is seriously sick. At least with us he's got health care, a warm place to sleep, three square meals a day. I don't get it. Is he just looking to die a free man? Where would he go?"

Avalyn peered out her window, "I wish I knew. It's like the world he lived in would not let him go, so he found a way. The entire world was focused on his death. And he gave them what they wanted: a controversy, a good show. Then having acted out the final scene, he just slipped off the stage. It's like we were all focused on his death but we were blinded to what he was really planning."

Within minutes, Avalyn could also see the metro bus about a half mile ahead, surrounded by the flow of urban traffic. She looked up at a green highway sign which read: CITY CENTER TUNNEL 1 MILE. Just then a city police car sped past them; Avalyn heard its siren rise and then fall in pitch as blue and red pulses of light flashed through the interior of the van as the patrol car raced past. This was soon followed by the rhythmic staccato of helicopter blades overhead. Avalyn peered upward out her window to see a police helicopter swoop to her right.

The radio lit up, "All units, be advised the subject vehicle, metro bus number fifty-seven, has entered the southbound city tunnel. The driver has been instructed to stop on the distant side of the tunnel. A blockade is in place."

Burke pressed the accelerator. Avalyn felt her body sink back into the seat. She could see the tunnel entrance but had lost site of the bus as it descended into the yellow fluorescent hues of the underpass.

As Burke and Avalyn descended into the tunnel, the stream of law enforcement radio transmissions became interrupted by static and the breaking up of words. The emergency channel continued to pick up intermittent updates from a series of transmission antennae along the ceiling of the tunnel, but many of the transmissions were broken up and garbled. Putting together the jigsaw of messages, Avalyn was able to make out that a road block had been established at the tunnel exit.

Halfway into the tunnel, the corrections van came upon the bright red brake lights of vehicles backed up in an underground traffic jam. Avalyn felt her body surge forward and then whiplash back as the lieutenant pressed hard on the brakes to avoid slamming into the rear of the small car in front of them.

Avalyn stretched her neck up to look ahead. She could see daylight illuminating the far end of the tunnel as it curved back up toward the surface, but the bus itself was not visible; all she could see was a double row of red tail-lights extending ahead of them from a mass of idling cars. The sounds of vehicles honking and people yelling echoed throughout the tunnel. Presumably the city bus had exited the tunnel and had been stopped by the authorities on the other side, essentially arresting all further movement of traffic.

Avalyn heard the troopers transmit a series of observations and reports as the response team boarded the bus to arrest Sherman. For a moment the radio went silent. Avalyn felt her blood momentarily pulse in her neck, then as if all the blood rushed from her head, she felt suddenly uneasy as she heard the final radio transmission, "Captain, the bus has been secured, every passenger has been identified and questioned; the suspect is not aboard the bus. The driver reports a man dressed in a blue uniform exited the bus while in traffic halfway through the tunnel. We believe the suspect may be still in the tunnel."

Burke keyed the microphone, "Dispatch, this is Lieutenant Burke with the Department of Corrections. I am currently located in the tunnel approximately three hundred yards from the exit."

Avalyn looked at Burke. Her face developed a puzzled tilt, "Do you think Sherman is still down here? Could he be in another car?"

A state trooper's voice came over the radio, "Lieutenant, this is Trooper Miller. Do you see any pedestrians from your vantage point?"

"Stand by. We will look." As Burke answered he rolled down his window to get a clear view of the tunnel around them.

Avalyn opened her window as well. As her window lowered, she heard what sounded like a violent rush of air, and she felt a simultaneous sinking of the van. Something in the rearview mirror caught her eye. She froze as the image became clear. With her left hand she began slapping at Lieutenant Burke's leg to get his attention. But he, with his head stretched out the driver's side window, did not recognize the non-verbal signal Avalyn was trying to convey. Words would not come out of her mouth. She watched in paralyzing horror as a man in a blue uniform stood up from the back tire and marched toward her window. Once Avalyn was able to draw a breath she screamed as if in a full body convulsion in which each syllable was emphasized by a tonic wave, "It-is-Sher-man!"

Joseph Sherman suddenly stood beside the open van window. He placed both hands on the passenger ledge as if to forcefully hold the window down, and he squinted his ominous eyes at Avalyn.

The lieutenant reached over Avalyn for Sherman, who initially appeared to be within arm's reach. But Sherman remained just out of the lieutenant's grasp, because Avalyn, who was visibly trembling in the passenger seat, had extended her feet to push herself away from Sherman. In doing so, she pushed the lieutenant back away from Sherman.

With his free hand, Lieutenant Burke fumbled for his

sidearm and raised it toward the open passenger window. He pointed the weapon at Sherman's chest and commanded, "Mr. Sherman, you are placing yourself and others in danger. Turn around and put your hands on the wall."

Avalyn saw the gun extended past her. She covered her ears anticipating a blast.

Sherman looked into the barrel of the handgun. He cocked his head as if first to study the weapon, and then he lifted his eyes to look directly at the lieutenant. A conniving broken grin grew across his face. Only the right corner of his mouth curled upward. Then he said in a low, slurred voice, "You can't threaten me with going home, Lieutenant. Now leave me in peace."

Sherman quickly turned and ran with an awkward, limping gait back along the sidewalk. After a few yards, he disappeared, having turned into a pedestrian exit on the tunnel wall.

The Lieutenant jumped from the van and ran after Sherman on foot, his weapon raised toward the exit door, yelling back at Avalyn, "Stay in the van. Do not come unless you're called out."

Avalyn ignored the order. She leapt from her side of the van and cautiously walked in the direction the lieutenant was running. She stopped, pausing at the back of the van, noting that the back tire had been slashed and that the van now sat at an awkward angle on the flattened tire. Avalyn stood there for a moment contemplating her predicament. She wavered between joining the pursuit and sitting in the van to wait it out. In that moment of shallow reflection, the background noise of horns and idling engines seemed to fade as Avalyn's fear gave way to a rising sense of audacity and clarity of thought. She reached into the side door of the van and picked up her emergency bag. Then she reached over the front seat to grab the radio microphone, "Uh, Troopers? This is Nurse Avalyn Robbins of the Department of Corrections. I'm in the tunnel. We located Mr. Sherman. He was just here but ran out a tunnel exit. Lieutenant Burke is chasing him on foot. I'm going to go after them with medical equipment. You might want to send someone up top."

"Copy that Nurse Robbins. Please do not pursue the suspect. Stay where you are."

Avalyn did not hear the directive. She had already turned to run, the emergency bag thrown over her shoulder, moving headlong toward and then through the tunnel exit door.

The tunnel exit opened first to a stairwell with steps leading upward to the street level, where an unmarked concrete structure sat at the edge of the city park. The structure looked like a small power station with a door on the side.

Avalyn burst through this door into the bright open air. She held a hand above her forehead, squinting against the sunlight and scanning the tree-lined park with its mixed scents of fresh-cut grass and blooming flowers. She looked for any sign of Lieutenant Burke or Sherman.

The park was filled with a mix of laughter, shouts, nearby traffic noise, and chirping birds. The two men, however, were not immediately visible.

A mass of people were gathered near the center of the park. Avalyn held the emergency bag firmly on her shoulder and walked briskly toward the crowd as pedestrians and joggers wove past her, moving in both directions.

As Avalyn drew near the crowd, she could see the people were circling a raised platform in the center of the park, a venue used by performers. The platform stood in the middle of a paved court which served as a hub from which park paths extended like spokes. The crowd had gathered to watch what appeared to be an act between two performers dressed as mimes competing with each other in dueling acts of bravery. Avalyn heard the crowd gasp in sudden fright and then burst into laughter as one of the mimes balanced in a handstand atop a stack of balanced chairs. Once the mime balanced himself in place, the crowd erupted into applause.

Avalyn scanned the crowd, bouncing on her toes to see above and then beyond the people on the edge of the crowd. *Where is he?* She derided herself for not moving faster.

Suddenly she felt a firm hand on her shoulder. She spun to see Lieutenant Burke standing behind her with a finger raised against his lips to indicate she should remain silent. He spoke in a hushed tone while looking around them, "I thought I said stay put. Sherman is somewhere here in the park. I saw him run toward this sideshow, but I lost him in the crowd. Follow me and keep your eyes open."

The two of them walked up to a grass-covered rise

on the park lawn from which they could view the entire park. Avalyn watched people pass for several minutes; then something caught her attention. She bumped the lieutenant with her elbow and pointed toward a man seated on a bench with his back to them. He was sitting about two hundred yards away. They both noticed the man was dressed in blue, leaning forward, holding what appeared to be a hat in his hands.

"It could be Sherman," said the lieutenant. He immediately but quietly edged toward the seated gentleman with a hand held over his holstered weapon as if ready to draw.

Avalyn was not so reserved. Either due to nerves or the general excitement of the moment, she cupped her hands over her mouth and yelled out, "Sherman."

At first no one seemed to hear her. The attention of the crowd was not swayed from the street performers, and pedestrians continued walk past, oblivious to Avalyn's call. But the man on the bench slowly placed an arm up on the back of the bench and turned to look. Avalyn thought, *Even in the crowded din of a city park, a man cannot resist the sound of his own name. We caught you, Sherman.*

Sherman first looked back toward the grass atop which Avalyn stood. His attention quickly shifted toward the lieutenant, who was now running toward him.

Sherman sprang to his feet. He held out his hat and bowed toward both Avalyn and Burke in a manner that acknowledged his pursuers and bid them farewell. Then he placed the hat on his head and ran into the crowd of people.

Avalyn did not give chase. She stood on the grass-covered rise from which she could see Lieutenant Burke chase Sherman into the crowd. She lost them in the midst of people but could discern their position as they pushed through the crowd by watching the movement of individuals erratically shifting to get out of the way.

Avalyn saw Sherman break free on the far side of the crowd. She noticed he ran with an awkward floppy gait as if one leg was timidly moving more slowly than the other. This struck her as odd. *What's wrong with him?* she thought.

A few seconds later, Lieutenant Burke broke free of the crowd and bolted toward Sherman in a full sprint with his weapon drawn shouting, "Sherman! Stop where you are!"

People jumped off the path and stood in amazement at the strange site of one law enforcement officer chasing down another law enforcement officer in broad daylight.

Avalyn could see Sherman weave his way across four lanes of traffic on the distant edge of the park, skillfully disappearing behind a bus stop. It was here that the lieutenant lost Sherman.

Avalyn peered forward with both hands over the sides of her eyes to block the ambient light and possibly get a clear view. She could see Burke pacing back and forth looking across the street. Neither of them could see Sherman.

After several minutes, Burke raised his arms in frustration. He turned and walked back toward Avalyn, who, seeing the lieutenant coming toward her, picked up the emergency bag and walked toward him as well. They met in front of the park bench where Sherman had just been sitting.

The lieutenant sat back onto the bench, still breathless from the pursuit. He leaned his head back toward the sky and reprimanded Avalyn, "What were you thinking, Robbins? I was so close. Don't they teach you nurses when to keep your mouth shut? I'll take care of security. You stick to medical care. Got it?"

"I'm really sorry, Lieutenant. I reacted without thinking. I did not think he'd up and run."

Avalyn dropped her bag to the ground and took a seat next to the Lieutenant. She avoided the urge to speak, preferring the momentary respite afforded by a park bench.

Lieutenant Burke leaned forward with his hands on his knees as he scanned the park. He continued to breathe heavily, his mouth open gulping large mouthfuls of air.

Avalyn noticed only a few pedestrians remained passing through the park; the park itself had quickly emptied of people presumably succumbing to a natural impulse to depart the scene of an armed chase.

Burke wiped the beads of sweat from his forehead and turned to Avalyn, "Explain to me how a man with terminal cancer can run like that. Look at me. I can't get my breath. My legs feel like gelatin. My knees are on fire. But my doc says I'm still in my prime. How could Sherman outrun me? I thought the guy was on death's doorstep. Is he just feigning the whole illness?"

Avalyn shook her head, but she did not immediately answer. She leaned back on the bench and looked up into the beams of light pouring through the intertwined limbs and leaves of the large park trees. The bench gave her body a chance to rest, but her mind raced through the events of the day. *How could an escaped prisoner with a terminal disease pull one woman's heart so wildly in so many directions?*

Then, after a few moments, Avalyn answered, "Yes, he has cancer. And yes, it's terminal. But Doctor Brant says there's no way to know when he'll go. He could make it another six months or he could die any day, maybe from a stroke or GI bleed or something. But for now, he has his strength."

"Well he's swift enough to give this old heart a workout."

"Should we contact the police or troopers?"

"I don't have a portable radio with me. We should just return to the van."

"He slashed the tire. The van is not much use to us."

"We don't need a tire, we need a radio. We can listen to the developments while we change the tire, or I'll call the facility to come with another van."

Avalyn and Burke rose from the bench and walked toward the tunnel access stairs. As they approached the street, a city police car pulled up to the curb beside them.

The officer, an overweight, dark-skinned man with a thick New England accent, rolled down his window and looked at the lieutenant with a smirk. With a playful laugh he said, "Now I'm not in the habit of giving rides to rent-a-cops, but you two look like you could use a ride."

Burke did not miss the opportunity to return the jest,

"So they let police drive cars now? The bicycle gig not working out for you? Where's your horse?"

Avalyn rolled her eyes at the interagency banter, "Don't you guys ever grow up?"

The police officer got out of the car and opened the back door, "Well let me show you how a real officer treats a lady. Hop in; we could use your help."

Avalyn tossed her bag onto the back seat and slid into the patrol car. Burke took the passenger seat up front.

The Lieutenant asked, "How did you know we were here?"

"Troopers said you called it in," answered the officer.

The lieutenant looked back at Avalyn. She shrugged and rolled her eyes, "Don't look at me. I'm just a nurse...just a nurse...who knows when to keep her mouth shut."

The lieutenant described their momentary contact with Sherman to the officer, who in turn transmitted the information to the dispatcher. As he gave the report, the three of them began patrolling the streets of downtown, systematically broadening a circular route extending outward from the central city park.

The radio transmissions fell mostly silent except for intermittent position reports from various officers and troopers. Avalyn felt her heavy eyes fighting off a tendency to sleep, lulled into somnolence by the steady hum of the patrol car engine and fatigue from the day's chaotic events.

Suddenly the radio erupted with abrupt, almost frantic reports from the dispatcher. Avalyn's heart skipped and then raced in a percussive blast. She became fully awake and fully alert. She leaned forward in her seat, "Please turn the radio up."

The officer reached up and increased the volume on the radio. The dispatcher spoke in stilted phrases, "All units, be advised: Mr. Joseph Sherman has been located. We have a positive identification. He is in the old Westminster Church."

CHAPTER EIGHTEEN

THE DIGNIFIED DEATH OF JOSEPH SHERMAN

"...it always amazes me to see that ours is a religion that allows a man to return to work at the last minute and still get full pay."

- Reuben Wallace
Westminster Church Deacon

The officer made an abrupt turn toward the Westminster Church building. Avalyn braced herself with an outstretched hand to avoid being pressed against the inside of the back seat door of the patrol car as it veered suddenly eastward with lights flashing and siren blaring.

From her window, Avalyn saw the silhouette of the Westminster Church rising like a historical stone backdrop against an otherwise modern cityscape about a mile south of the city park. She bent forward to speak with the officer and lieutenant through the cage-like barrier of the patrol car, "Is Sherman still in the church? I did not hear the entire transmission. Did they say they had him in custody? How fast can you get us to that church?"

The sun had set, and the road had collected a thin layer of water from a gentle evening rain. A rising white mist seemed to trail the vehicle as it sped through traffic. The billowing mist reflected and magnified the patrol car's flashing blue and red lights. Avalyn sat on her hands and peered ahead like an anxious child amazed by the sight of other vehicles separating before the police car.

A collection of law enforcement vehicles, a TV station van, and at least one ambulance were already parked in front of the church building. The lights from the emergency vehicles reflected off the wet stone walls in flashes which gave the entire structure the appearance of a large sparkling stained glass window.

The officer parked in the midst of the other vehicles. Lieutenant Burke threw open his door and reached back to open the back door for Avalyn. She grabbed the emergency supply bag and stepped out of the car. Together they ran up the stone steps of the church through a gathered crowd of curious onlookers and news reporters.

One news reporter stood in front of the large wooden arched doorway, her blond hair illuminated by a light mounted on the shoulder of her camera man. As Avalyn passed, she heard the reporter saying something about the death of an escaped convict.

Then Avalyn heard a police officer telling a group of reporters who were pressing against the entrance, "Back off, people. This is a house of worship, not a news studio."

The officer noticed the badges worn by Avalyn and Lieutenant Burke, and he waved them through the doorway. Avalyn followed the leiutenant through a low-ceilinged narthex, which in turn opened into a cavernous sanctuary.

Two paramedics passed Avalyn and Burke, carrying large medical duffel bags and pushing an empty wheeled gurney out of the sanctuary, their heads respectfully bowed. They acknowledged Avalyn and Burke with only a momentary nod.

Avalyn gave the lieutenant an inquisitive glance as if to ask, *Why are they leaving?* But the lieutenant continued forward into the sanctuary, undeterred by either the paramedics' or Avalyn's puzzled looks. He continued ahead of Avalyn to the front of the church.

Avalyn entered the sanctuary and suddenly stopped, partially out of reverence, but more from a sudden need to calm her nerves. She took a deep, slow breath and tried to consciously slow her pounding heart. Her attempt to calm herself seemed to have the opposite effect. Her pulse increased both in rate and intensity. For a moment she could not move.

The church sanctuary was designed like a traditional cathedral, with internal lines intended to draw a person's eyes forward and upward to a focal point, a large cross displayed on the anterior wall. On the cross hung the statue of an emaciated, crucified man, his fallen countenance looking down upon the platform.

A gathering of law enforcement officers and curious onlookers stood around the front, most of them speaking with each other in hushed, reverent tones.

Avalyn summoned enough strength to walk about halfway down the aisle. Then she saw something which appeared ominously still in the midst of an otherwise mingling crowd. The sight made Avalyn instantly weak. She leaned against the end of a wooden pew to keep from falling to her knees.

In the center of the platform, below the foot of the cross, Avalyn could see the flaccid shape of a man lying motionless under what appeared to be a heavy green sheet. She felt a dry knot form in her throat, making it hard to swallow. Tears obscured her view of the man, but she knew what she was seeing. The emergency bag fell from her shoulder to the floor as her heart sank. She whispered, "Oh, dear God, not like this, please not here."

The lieutenant turned from speaking with a police officer to see Avalyn slowly walking down the aisle. She was wiping her eyes and reaching forward to hold the edges of the pews as if she needed support with each step. Lieutenant Burke met her halfway, "You don't look well, Robbins."

"Is it him? Is it Sherman?"

"Yes. He has passed. The police were called here about thirty minutes ago. One of the church staff found him."

Avalyn felt the piercing pain of unwanted news. She placed a hand on her chest, "May we see him?"

The lieutenant nodded and took her by the arm, escorting her through a crowded mix of law enforcement and curious onlookers to the spot where Mr. Sherman lay in silence under the thick green cloth.

They stood over the body for several minutes, thoughtful, in respectful quiet, staring at the contour of a covered corpse. Avalyn then looked around at the ornate, sacred setting, wondering why had he come to a church. Did he come to make his peace? Did he think that taking the pills before God would lend some sacred credibility to his decision? Or was his intent something altogether spiteful? Was this his way of firmly expressing disbelief? Did he take the pills here as a final shaking of the fist at an omnipotent being as if to say here is what I think of your so-called life? Or was he putting God to the test, a way of asking if you are the Almighty, only you can save me now?

Avalyn looked at the lieutenant and whispered, "Who found him? How did he get in here?"

The lieutenant pointed toward one side of the podium, "Do you see the man speaking with the trooper? He was here when it happened. The trooper says he is one of the leaders or deacons or something to that effect."

Avalyn looked across the sanctuary. A state trooper was interviewing a middle-aged man with a red curly beard and balding head. He was wearing a brown, poorly-fitting sport coat that hung a little too long on his arms and square rim glasses which gave him the appearance of a professor or clergy. The trooper gave the gentlemen his full attention while simultaneously scribbling notes in a small, black flip notebook as the gentleman spoke.

When the trooper noticed Lieutenant Burke approaching with Avalyn, he stopped the interview to introduce each of them to each other, "This is Mr. Wallace, a deacon at Westminster. He was in the church at the time of Sherman's death."

Mr. Wallace continued speaking in a distinctive foreign accent, perhaps British, South African, or Australian in origin, "As I was saying, the man had been kneeling there for over an hour. It's not unusual for people to stop in to pray in the afternoon or on the way home from work. So we leave the church open, you see. I presumed he was some kind of police officer or security person and had stopped in either coming from or going to work. I don't recall seeing him before. I don't believe he's part of the congregation. But visitors are always welcome and not an unusual sight. He was a different sort, I admit. Most people just come and sit in one of the pews. But I guess he had something on his mind; he stayed right there, up front on his knees, looking up the whole time."

The trooper interrupted, "Did he speak to you or anyone else?"

"No, we did not speak. Although at one point I approached him, you know, to let him know I'd be locking up the church in a bit, and I overheard his words. His prayer was most unusual, I thought. So I refrained and did not interrupt him but just left him for a few more minutes. When I returned, he was gone, I mean just slumped over and not breathing. That's when I called for emergency services."

The trooper continued to write, "And what time was that exactly?"

"Must have been close to six o'clock. That's when we close for the evening."

Avalyn followed the conversation up until that point. She had questions of her own, which she did not sense were inappropriate to interject. So she broke into the interview, "Excuse me. I'm sorry to interrupt, but what did he say that was unusual?"

The gentleman gave her a kind, inquisitive look over the top of his glasses, "Well he repeated the same phrase over and over. He just said, 'Remember me.' He repeated that phrase over and over, 'Remember me…Remember me.' It was a strange prayer for a guy like him I thought."

The lieutenant asked, "Why do you say it was

strange?"

"Well he's clearly a uniformed officer of the law; but that's the prayer of a dying criminal."

"You're not serious?" asked Avalyn.

"I'm quite serious, I can assure you."

"How did you know that he was a criminal?"

"Well, I did not mean to imply that he is a criminal. I just mean that the prayer he prayed was a criminal's prayer, the supplication of a dying thief to be exact." Mr. Wallace noticed the others looking at him without the slightest idea of what he meant, "Doesn't anyone read the Bible anymore? Two criminals on crosses were dying on either side of Jesus of Nazareth. Each of them prayed to Jesus. One selfishly demanded proof of Christ's deity while the other, a penitent, prayed for eternal pardon. 'Jesus, remember me when you come into your kingdom,' he said."

Avalyn suddenly felt very sad and a not just a little used. She looked back toward the draped body. *Did Sherman come to ask for forgiveness? Did he orchestrate the whole thing to end up here on the day of his death? Was this his plan all along?*

Lieutenant Burke said to the gentleman, "Did you know this man escaped from the prison today?"

"I most certainly did not. How could I have known such a thing?"

The lieutenant pointed toward the podium, "That man is Joseph Sherman, or it was Joseph Sherman. He's a convicted murderer. Earlier today, he poisoned a corrections officer and disguised himself in the officer's uniform to escape."

Mr. Wallace placed a hand over his heart, "So, that is Joe Sherman? The murderer no less? Imagine that. Waiting until the last minute to seek a pardon."

The deacon's face suddenly took on a full-faced smile, and then he broke into a genuine laugh. It was the kind of laugh that seems to feed itself, growing in a sort of crescendo of giggles, causing tears of joy and a momentary loss of the ability to breathe, ending finally after a deep high-pitched breath and a relaxing sigh. He patted his hand on the lieutenant's shoulder and said, "I'm sorry, my friend. Perhaps this is not a laughing matter to you. But it always amazes me to see that ours is a religion that allows a man to return to work at the last minute and still get full pay."

The lieutenant reflexively pulled his shoulder back; he did not smile but said in a professional manner, "We have reason to believe he proceeded here to take his own life."

"I did not witness any behavior consistent with suicide or a suicidal gesture. All I know is the man was praying, and then he died."

"Did you notice him taking anything such as medication or a drink?"

"I did not. Every time I saw him he had his hands folded in front of him.

Avalyn was still looking toward the body trying to envision what went through Sherman's mind in his final moments. *Did he take the pills? Did he suffer? Perhaps his life was taken from him before he was able to take the medication.* She turned toward the lieutenant and asked, "May I remove the sheet? I feel like I need to see him. It sounds strange, but I just need to be sure."

"You're the medical one. I'll just keep my distance if you don't mind. We are waiting on the medical examiner to take possession of the body."

Avalyn walked back and squatted next to Sherman's body. She lifted the upper portion of the green sheet to uncover the head and upper torso. The face was that of Joseph Sherman, his eyes partially open with pupils fixed and dilated in a shock-like gaze, his mouth still open as if his final words were yet to be spoken.

Avalyn felt a sudden sense of sorrow. She raised the back of her hand over her open mouth and softly spoke the words, "I'm so sorry, Mr. Sherman." Later she would say that her emotional response was not out of compassion for Joseph Sherman; he was a murderous manipulator with a legacy for adding to the net suffering in the world. She felt no compassion for him in particular, but she felt a general sense of remorse that any human being, whether good or evil, had to die alone.

Before standing up, Avalyn reached forward to reposition Sherman. It was her custom to prepare a deceased patient for viewing by cleaning the face and placing the arms in a relaxed position across the abdomen. She had no way of really preparing Sherman. She had no cloth to wash his face or wipe his mouth. Instead she smoothed his skin with the palm of her hand and straightened his neck from its contorted position. She could feel a trace of moist body heat retained in Sherman's skin, but overall, he felt cool to the touch.

Avalyn then reached forward to pull Sherman's arms across his body. As she grabbed his arm she felt something stiff under his lower shirt just above the belt line. She quickly pulled back more of the sheet to locate the object. It was under his buttoned shirt, hidden from view just underneath the belt-line. It was a rectangular item with sharp edges.

She unbuttoned the lower part of the shirt and found not just a single item, but three identical cards, the medication bubble sheets. The sight of the cards momentarily took her breath. How many did he take? She bent closer and lifted the cards carefully one by one, holding each by the corner as if she was lifting a valuable piece of evidence from a crime scene. As she raised the cards, she peered closely at the contents of each one.

Avalyn's hands were shaking, "Lieutenant, come here. You've got to see this." The cards were almost completely intact. But eight pills were missing. Avalyn's heart sank and she began to cry, "He must have taken a handful and just gone to sleep."

The lieutenant knelt next to her and awkwardly placed an arm around Avalyn's shoulder, "Robbins, I have to tell you something. I just got a call from the prison. They found the inmate who helped Sherman escape. It was Blaine Russell. He still had five of the capsules in his possession."

Avalyn leaned into the lieutenant's chest. She could not speak in the sudden release of pent up grief. Tears flowed from her eyes. She was shaking. Her nose was running. And her breathing was erratically interrupted by involuntary sobs. She finally looked up, "So, Mr. Sherman did not kill himself? Is it true? I'm so thankful. Forgive me for saying this, I'm just so relieved."

The lieutenant took the pill cards and stood up. He walked them over to a state trooper who placed the pills in an evidence bag. The lieutenant then returned to Avalyn, who was still squatting at Sherman's side. He bent down and asked, "So what do you think got him? How did he die, if not by taking the pills?"

Avalyn wiped tears away with the palm of her hand, "I can't say; maybe a stroke or something." She glanced upward, "God only knows. They will have to perform an autopsy to find the real answer."

Within a few minutes, the medical examiner arrived with a team of assistants to take possession of Sherman's body.

The lieutenant stood and patted Avalyn on the back, "Time to go."

Avalyn stood up to follow, but after a few steps, she stopped and walked back to Sherman's body. She bent down next to him and took a deep breath. Then she reached out her hand and closed Sherman's eyes and mouth. While doing this, she whispered a blessing of sorts, "I do not know the manner of your death, Mr. Sherman, but may God find you to have died with dignity and grant you peace."

CHAPTER NINETEEN

FOR THE GOOD

"There's nothing dignified about death. Let's enjoy life for a bit, shall we?"

\- Avalyn Robbins, RN
Prison Nurse

Avalyn took a taxi back to the prison parking lot while Lieutenant Burke returned to the highway tunnel to repair and retrieve the state van.

Avalyn went straight to her car. Her shift had ended, and her thoughts centered on returning to her children and husband. But before going home, she had a final stop to make. She pulled out of the prison parking lot and drove her car toward the hospital.

The city's memorial hospital was a sprawling medical complex near downtown, set on a hill that overlooked much of the city. As Avalyn approached the facility, she thought the hospital itself appeared peaceful in the glow of street lights. Avalyn pulled into the largely empty parking lot and entered through an entrance marked with large, red, illuminated letters, EMERGENCY.

Just inside the automatic glass doors, Avalyn met a thin lady with streaks of pink hair sitting behind an information desk in the emergency room lobby. The receptionist quickly lowered her feet from the desk, momentarily alarmed by Avalyn's walking through the door. She looked up from behind a glass window and greeted Avalyn in a manner that would have seemed professional were it not for the conspicuous way in which she chewed her gum while speaking, "May I help you this evening?"

"Yes, my name is Avalyn Robbins. I'm here to see a patient."

"Name?"

"His name is Frantz Vatel. He was brought in several hours ago by ambulance."

The attendant looked at her computer screen and typed in an impatient fashion, using the enter key incessantly as if it where the designated stress relief button for a slowly responding computer. Finally she looked up again and pointed toward a windowed office marked SECURITY located next to a double door entrance into the emergency room, "Mr. Vatel is still here in the emergency department. Room twenty-six. You may speak with security for a pass to see him."

Avalyn obtained a sticker labeled VISITOR from the security officer with her name printed in a small font, and she proceeded through the automatic double doors into the emergency department. Her eyes initially strained against the sudden glare of bright fluorescent overhead lights, and she felt the sudden chill of the cool air of the emergency wing. A nurse in blue scrubs pointed her toward room twenty-six.

The speakers overhead repeated apathetic announcements for doctors to call this or that number. Physically exhausted people in white coats and scrubs passed by as Avalyn made her way through the emergency department. The bustle took Avalyn's memory back to her days in nursing school when these sounds and smells and palpable anxiety catalyzed with caffeine completely filled her waking hours.

As Avalyn approached room twenty-six, a young resident with disheveled black hair and dark circles under his eyes was walking out of the room. Avalyn gently grabbed the sleeve of his white coat, "Excuse me, Doctor. Is this the room for Mr. Vatel? He is a friend."

"Yes ma'am. You have the correct room."

"May I ask his condition?"

The young doctor looked both ways as if preparing to share a secret. Then he looked right at Avalyn, disarmed by her direct manner and nursing attire, "He remains sleepy but otherwise awake and alive. Lucky man. Sounds like a prisoner tried to do him in. But the dose of medication he received was relatively low. He swallowed enough to make him go to sleep, but not enough to depress his respiratory drive. You must be his nurse? You may go in."

Avalyn pushed the curtain to the side and peered into the room. Vatel was lying in a hospital bed with the head slightly raised. He was wearing a thin, poorly fitting gown, asleep with his mouth open, breathing deeply, on the edge of snoring. Avalyn watched for a moment. She instinctively looked at the vital signs and heart rhythm display and noted the rate at which IV fluid dripped into Vatel's arm.

Avalyn said, "Good evening, Officer."

Vatel took a stuttered waking breath and opened his eyes. Partially dazed, he studied Avalyn from across the small room and then responded, "Well, hello, Mrs. Robbins. Guess you caught me sleeping on the job. Come on in. I'm glad they let you come in here."

"How are you, Vatel?"

"I feel great, like you feel after a good Sunday afternoon nap; you know, content but a little fuzzy in the head. They say I'll be here under observation until morning. Doctor says I was drugged with those sleeping pills you gave Mr. Sherman. But I didn't take any pills, Mrs. Robbins. You know I'm straight and would never take pills from anyone."

"Vatel, don't worry. No one has accused you of taking medication from inmates."

"I wish I knew how it happened. Strange, I don't remember much. I remember going into Mr. Sherman's room. He wanted to speak to me about something. He said he wanted to make amends. Asked me to forgive him and even said thank you. Then I remember a sudden urge to lie down, like I was falling out of my body. That's it, that's all I remember. Now I hear he's escaped. The police were by here earlier. They said Sherman made off wearing my uniform."

"It's true. Sherman drugged you and was on the run most of the day."

"They caught him then?"

"Vatel, I have to tell you: Sherman is dead."

"Oh, Mrs. Robbins, rest that man's soul, how did it happen? Did he take his own life? Did he hurt someone else? Did the police kill him?"

"We don't know what killed him. He just died. He was found slumped over in the old Westminster Church."

"Did he take those pills you gave him? Did he go through with it? I sure wanted to snatch those cards right out of his hands when I saw how much it burdened you, Mrs. Robbins. Tell me he didn't do it."

For some reason, Vatel's genuine concern touched Avalyn. Her lip quivered and a single tear descended from the corner of her eye, "No, Vatel. He just died. He just made his peace and passed on. Maybe he died from a stroke or something. We don't know. But the pills were still in the packages. He did not take any of them."

Vatel sat upright in the bed. He crossed his arms and looked at Avalyn, "It's better this way, Mrs. Robbins, not knowing the cause. Forgive me for saying this, but being the cause of a man's death would have been a terrible burden to bear."

Avalyn grabbed a tissue from a bedside stand, "Thank you, Vatel. I do feel like that burden has lifted."

They continued to talk for several minutes; Avalyn filled Vatel in on the events of the day, and Vatel listened intently, asking questions and tossing in a story or two of his own from his somnolent misadventure to the emergency room. When the conversation came around to a natural pause, Vatel leaned back in the bed and looked at the ceiling and said, "Thank you for coming, Mrs. Robbins. It sure does mean a lot to me. But you need to get home to your family. Officer Robbins and those children are lucky to have you."

Avalyn departed the hospital and drove home. Rush hour had long since passed, and traffic was light, making the commute home reasonably short. Avalyn sat in her car alone in her driveway for a few minutes, allowing the day's events to filter into the recesses of her mind while she simultaneously prepared herself to walk through the front door and be fully present as a mother and wife.

As she cracked open the front door, Avalyn paused. She dropped her satchel and smiled at the thought of what predictably came next. First she heard the approach of pounding little feet accompanied by voices yelling, "Mommy!" Then a little boy and his little sister came running, and each in turn leapt into the air without hesitation, fully trusting a soft landing in their mother's arms.

Holding a chattering child in each arm, Avalyn proceeded to the kitchen. As she rounded the corner, her husband looked up from cutting vegetables for a salad. His eyes lit up at the sight of Avalyn, and he smiled a welcoming smile. "Ave, you made it. Come eat dinner," he said. "It's late, and you must be exhausted."

Avalyn lowered the children to the ground and gave her husband a kiss while the children giggled and clung to her legs.

Her husband laid down the kitchen knife. He turned to embrace Avalyn. Then he placed his hands on either side of her face and said, "I was worried about you. Did things turn out ok?"

Avalyn smiled and looked up at her hero. She felt secure in his arms, protected from the stress of her work and the persistent pull of weighty, competing interests. The tension in her shoulders subsided as the burdens of the day seemed to fall away like a heavy bag dropped to the floor at the end of a hard journey. Her eyes became moist. She leaned into her husband and buried her head into his chest, "I'm ok now."

"We heard there was an escape from the complex. They said it was Sherman. Did you get pulled into that too? The news just reported he was found dead."

Avalyn nodded but she cut her eyes down toward the children as if to indicate that the conversation was not appropriate for their young ears. Then she answered cryptically, "It was a difficult day for all of us. I'll let you in on the details later."

Her husband took the hint and returned to making the salad. But as he scooped the cut vegetables into a wooden bowl he could not resist asking one more question in a somewhat euphemistic tone, "So about our man in the infirmary, did you make it back to him in time? Or did he end up, you know, dying with dignity as they say?"

Avalyn was carrying a stack of plates to the table. She lowered the plates to the table and walked back to the counter. Lifting the wooden salad bowl, she leaned forward to whisper into her husband's ear, "There's nothing dignified about death. Let's enjoy life for a bit, shall we?"

Within a few minutes the young family was sitting around the table eating, laughing, and telling stories in an evening ritual that fed little mouths and fortified young minds.

Avalyn leaned back in her chair. She looked around the table at her attentive husband and sloppy-faced children, the people that meant the most to her. She thought of her friends. She thought of Vatel. She thought of the chaplain. She said a silent prayer for Doctor Brant. And she thought for a moment about the death of Joseph Sherman. Then she smiled with her eyes, as only eyes can smile, and she said softly to herself, "I see it now; there was a reason for today, and it has worked out for the good.

ABOUT THE AUTHOR

Robert T. Lawrence, MD is a physician who lives, works, and writes in Anchorage, Alaska.

Inquiries? Questions for the author?
Contact us at our website:

www.willowptarmiganpress.com

Willow Ptarmigan Press
Anchorage, Alaska